Donald Macdonald is a p
He has had a successful and varied theatrical
has taken him around the world. He is also a prize-winning film writer. His now classic play, *Caravan*, continues to be one of the most successful comedies ever produced in Australia, as well as having had productions in the United Kingdom and New Zealand.

TRAVELS *with a* WISE MAN

Donald Macdonald

PAN
Pan Macmillan Australia

First published 1995 in Pan by Pan Macmillan Australia Pty Limited
St Martins Tower, 31 Market Street, Sydney

National Library of Australia
cataloguing-in-publication data:

Macdonald, Donald (Donald James).
Travels with a wise man.
ISBN 0 330 35649 6.
I. Title.
A823.3

Typeset in 10½/13 Bembo by Midland Typesetters
Printed in Australia by McPhersons Printing Group

For Nelly, Mac, and all those who helped me along the way.

1

Last night I dreamt I met a Wise Man . . .

It was the beginning of a journey that would take me into another world. An uncharted world, mysterious and magical. There I would meet the Wise Man. And I would find myself.

I didn't know this as I lay in that strange time between sleep and dreams. Odd, the images the mind can present in that state. Faces floated in and out of my consciousness. People and places I had never seen before.

What would happen if I just watched the pictures in my mind? Where would they lead me?

I found myself suddenly fully dressed and standing in a dark cavern. I edged forward curiously. The floor of the cavern fell away and a ladder on the rock wall beneath my feet disappeared into a golden light. Enjoying my adventure, I began to climb down.

As I came closer to the light I wanted to jump into the vast golden glow, it was very inviting. A voice within told me to jump. So I did.

I drifted like a feather, down through the light. I was one with its energy. A wonderful joy filled my being and

I thought I would burst from sheer happiness.

With a bump, I landed on the cavern floor. Ahead of me were two caves. I was standing near a pool. There was something in the pool. I couldn't see it but I knew it was there and I was afraid.

Two huge eyes slowly appeared above the surface. Ghastly, bloodshot eyes. I couldn't move. They held me in their dreadful gaze, watching me without blinking. A huge snout, filled with sharp yellow teeth and bigger than my arm, dripping with saliva, rose out of the water and lunged at me. I screamed.

It was a very, very big dragon.

I didn't believe in dragons. This was only a dream.

If you've ever had a nightmare where you were paralysed with fear, even though you were dreaming, then you'll know what I experienced.

I was dragged under the water by the hideous creature. I screamed and struggled, swallowing a lot of water, and gasping for breath. The dragon's great snout released me, only to breathe fire on me. The power of the beast's breath blew me back out of the water. Sobbing with fear, I staggered to the entrance of the nearest cave.

It was dark in there. I sensed other creatures in the cave and I didn't want to meet them. I crept towards the cave on my right, where there was a light. I hovered uncertainly at the entrance.

Behind me, the giant dragon drew itself out of the water and shook itself, its huge tail swishing. The wind from this movement, almost blew me into the cave. The dragon sat watching me with its hypnotic eyes.

My only escape was into the cave. I followed the path towards the light. Soon the cave was filled with a light so bright I could hardly see. I stumbled through the light, and fell into a room. The incredible brightness faded. I blinked and rubbed my eyes. I stood before a throne, and on it was a man.

He had long, dark hair, a beard, and black shining eyes that seemed to pierce through me. His powerful presence filled the room and he could have been quite frightening but he smiled at me gently, as though he had been expecting me.

He beckoned me impatiently to come forward.

'Why do you run away from your fears?' he asked.

He spoke in the kindly, rather irritated tones of a parent who knew me well and wouldn't be shocked by anything I did. I felt immediately that this man *did* know me better than I knew myself. I didn't like the feeling but I was sure he could see into my soul.

'I was running away from the dragon,' I replied breathlessly.

'Oh, pshaw! It is only when you face your fears that they go away,' he said, ignoring my remark about the dragon.

Though he seemed irritated with me, there was such a strong sense of love coming from him that I wasn't afraid. My heart lifted. I was like a child in the presence of a loving father.

'Was the dragon the fear I'm running from?'

'Now you're getting it,' said the man.

'Who are you?' I asked.

'I've been waiting for you for a long while. It is time. Come.'

He led me back through the cave, towards the dragon. Those baleful eyes glared at me through half-closed slits.

The dragon had been sleeping and we'd woken him.

'You have to go past him to get out of here. You might as well face him.' The man pushed me towards the dragon. 'Give him a pat.'

I was terrified but I did as I was told and patted the dragon on his haunch. He stared at me loftily, then yawned. His horrible breath blew me backwards.

'See? That wasn't so bad,' said the man.

I looked, and the dragon had gone.

The Wise Man, as I had already begun to call him in my mind, grinned at me, amused.

'If I'm only dreaming this, I could have made the dragon go away, anyway,' I said with false bravado, remembering how frozen with fear I had been earlier.

'Exactly,' snorted the Wise Man. 'Why didn't you think of that before.'

Then he clicked his fingers and disappeared.

Suddenly, I was standing in the courtyard of what appeared to be a castle, and a child was there. A sturdy little blond boy of about six or seven, who wore a shirt, shorts and sandals that were very out of fashion. He had his back towards me and was sobbing uncontrollably.

'What's wrong?' I asked.

'You don't love me,' the child wailed.

I was puzzled. To my knowledge I'd never seen him before. Yet when he turned to me with his blond curly hair, large dark eyes and solemn expression, he reminded me of myself at that age.

'Who are you?' I asked. 'Do I know you?'

At this, the child became even more upset. I was forced to take him in my arms. He cheered up considerably and hugged me, his little arms around my neck, his face beaming with pleasure.

'Can I come with you?' he said.

'Where?'

'On our travels, dumb-dumb,' said the Wise Man, appearing behind me and giving me a start. I stared at him uncomprehendingly.

'When you're ready, of course,' said the Wise Man.

'Where are we going?'

'You'll find out as we go along.'

The child still clung to me. He was heavy, so I put him down. 'Who is he?' I asked, as he still held on to my hand.

'Your Inner Child,' said the Wise Man. 'You've ignored him for too long.'

I looked at the Child. Was he really me? No wonder he seemed familiar.

'We'll take him with us,' the Wise Man continued. 'And you'll make notes. It is time for you to write stories that contain the truth. It'll be easier for people to understand than all these self-help books they read.'

I stared at the Wise Man, then at the Child. The Wise Man waited.

'So? Are you ready?' he said finally.

'I don't know.' I don't like to be hurried. I felt I was being pushed into this and I wasn't at all certain I wanted to be.

The Wise Man sighed heavily, as though he was dealing with an idiot.

'Let me know when you are,' he said with an exaggerated show of patience. 'But . . .' his dark eyes gleamed a warning, 'don't delay too long. There's not much time.'

He took the Child's hand and they walked away. The Child waved a sad little farewell. I felt I'd let them down badly.

The Wise Man turned back, grinning wickedly. I was sure he was enjoying my discomfort.

He winked and said, 'By the way, we'll call the book, "Travels with a Wise Man".'

He smiled again, and I woke up.

2

LAST NIGHT I DREAMT I MET A WISE MAN . . .

I wrote the words down in my diary and made a few notes. I laughed at myself. This was ridiculous. What on earth did the Wise Man expect me to write? Anyway, he was only in my mind. I didn't have to take what he said seriously.

Yet the experience had been so vivid. During my waking hours I couldn't forget the Wise Man or his warning. There wasn't much time left to do what we had to do. Whatever that was!

The second time I met the Wise Man he was sitting in the sunlight outside his cave by a stream surrounded with trees.

I had tried halfheartedly a few nights to contact him but I decided perhaps I was going mad, attempting to talk to a figment of my imagination. And so I'd fall asleep.

I began to be depressed. On the night I met him again, I went to bed with pains in the stomach, brought on, I was sure, by my negative thinking over the last few days.

I lay in bed, closed my eyes and tried to climb down

the ladder to the cavern. This time I didn't fall asleep. The hole of light appeared at my feet.

I took a deep breath, jumped into the light and found myself before the Wise Man.

'Nice of you to drop by again.' He sat cross-legged by the stream, his piercing eyes glaring at me. He, of course, wasn't at all surprised to see me.

'How are you feeling?'

'I haven't been feeling very well, as a matter of fact,' I answered.

'Oh, pshaw! Tut-tut.' He was most unsympathetic. 'If you got busy doing what you should be doing instead of being negative, negative, then you wouldn't get sick.' He waved a hand impatiently in my face. 'Sit, sit.'

He pushed me down roughly and ran his hands over my body without actually touching me, as though testing for the negatives. He stopped at my stomach. He mumbled something darkly to himself and then sent light to that area. I could see the light coming from his hands and I could feel it doing me good.

'What should I be doing?' I knew I shouldn't have asked that question.

'Knucklehead!' he yelled. He knocked on the top of my skull with his knuckles. It hurt.

'Now clean off,' he ordered, nodding towards the stream. My heart gave a little leap of fear. I wondered if the dragon, or something worse, was waiting there. Was this another test?

'What's wrong?' asked the Wise Man innocently.

'Nothing.'

The waters of the stream were crystal clear. There was nothing visible below the surface. I leapt in. Immediately my whole body was filled with light and I felt transformed in some way. I emerged from the water happier than I had been for some time.

'Now go and see the Child,' said the Wise Man.

I was returned to the castle, and there was the Child, sitting alone, his back to me. He was less distracted than before but still reluctant to talk to me.

I persuaded him to come and embrace me and managed to get a smile from him.

'You won't leave me again?' he begged. I still didn't fully understand who he was or why he believed I had deserted him.

The Wise Man appeared behind me, again giving me a start.

'He is a side of you that you have always neglected,' he told me, reading my thoughts. 'The Inner Child that needs to be loved and encouraged. Who never grew up because he suffered when you were a child, and who has remained in sadness all this time. It is up to you to nurture him and encourage him to grow until he is a harmonious part of you.'

The Wise Man stared at me as though waiting for me to say something.

All I could say was 'Thank you.'

'When are we going?' he asked.

'Where?'

'On our travels.'

'When you're ready, I suppose,' I replied, not at all sure what to say.

'No. When *you're* ready!' he shouted. 'How much longer do we have to wait?' His eyes were deep pools of darkness. The Child gave me a sorrowful and accusing look. The Wise Man glared at me.

'And you'd better hurry up,' he warned once again. 'Time is running out.' He and the Child walked away.

'How will I know when I'm ready?' I shouted after them helplessly. There was so much more I wanted to know. But the Wise Man had done his disappearing trick again. Then I was awake, and lying in bed.

I patted my stomach. It really was better. I felt alive and energised, and certainly not able to sleep. I lay awake for hours, pondering what the Wise Man had said.

I wondered when we would make the mythical journey he talked about. When would I be ready?

3

THE NEXT TIME THE WISE MAN FOUND *ME*. I WENT TO bed and closed my eyes. And he was immediately there, in front of my eyes, beckoning.

It had been some time since I had visited him but I hadn't stopped thinking about him. The so-called real world had started to be very dull. My visits to the Wise Man were more vivid than any waking experience. And though I laughed and tried to convince myself it was all in my imagination, I had to admit to feelings of guilt. I hadn't started to write 'Travels with a Wise Man' as he had told me I should.

Even if the Wise Man was only some aspect of my subconscious, as a writer I was being helped. I'd been given the idea and the title for a book and told to go ahead and write it.

But what journey were we supposed to make?

His words, 'Time is running out', worried me and yet I couldn't think how to begin the book. I had never written anything remotely like this. Who was I to write a book of spiritual truths?

'Because I asked you to, dummy,' the Wise Man said

angrily as he appeared before my eyes. In a flash I was down in the cavern and he was sitting cross-legged at the edge of the pool.

He wore a beige sarong and a shirt in the same colour. His skin was brown and with his long hair and beard he looked like a mad Indian Holy Man, which perhaps he was. His dark eyes gleamed with humour, and sudden anger.

He beckoned me to sit down beside him, which I did. He stared at me, making me feel uncomfortable. I was sure he could read my thoughts. I waited for him to speak, but he didn't.

Finally, to break the silence, I asked: 'When do we begin our travels?'

He smiled, then laughed mirthlessly. 'I should be asking you that question. We have waited here many days but you never came.'

'I'm sorry, I've been very busy and . . . ' My voice faded away at the look in his eyes. I didn't believe my own excuses. I should have come sooner.

'I'm ready when you are,' I said lamely.

'Good, I thought you'd never ask.'

He leapt up and motioned me to stand too. He glared at me again, staring at me darkly, or rather, staring into me, then he held up his hands. His palms, I noted, were remarkably smooth and unlined.

He ran his hands over me as he had done before. I immediately felt lighter, as though he had cleansed me in some way. I was grinning happily. At the same time he was mumbling'Psst! Psst!' and waving his hands as though hitting something away from me. Was it my imagination or were there little dark clouds moving away from my body? As I watched, the clouds floated upwards and became several small bats flying away into the darkness of the cave on the left.

'Dark thoughts,' he said and rubbed his hands together as though cleansing them of my dirt.

'Mine?' I asked.

'Who else, dumb-dumb.' The Wise Man strode on ahead to the lighted cave on the right. I hesitated.

'Come, come,' he shouted impatiently. I hurriedly followed.

We entered the brightness of the cave. My heart lifted as the light filled my being. I looked down and the Child was at my side, holding my hand.

He smiled up at me. The Wise Man smiled too.

'So,' he said. 'We begin our travels.'

4

I RELUCTANTLY BEGAN MY TRAVELS WITH THE WISE Man.

I had no idea what I was getting into, and if I had known I probably would never have agreed to go. But, on looking back, I didn't really have any choice. Despite my misgivings I felt impelled to go along with the Wise Man and the Child on their journey.

Once I had made the decision I was quite light-hearted. I laughed at the Child's enthusiasm as we followed the Wise Man through the Cave of Light.

The light was fading. When we reached the far end of the cave there was another entrance, through which only a glimmer of pale sunlight fell.

We walked from the cave into the midday sun and found ourselves in a strange, desolate landscape. I began to have forebodings.

We were at the edge of a harsh, dry valley. It wasn't inviting. An ominous, grey craggy cliff rose above us on the left, and to the right, at the bottom of the path we were on, there was a single, large tree overhanging a stream. There were no other trees. Desert stretched endlessly. The air was heavy and still and the sun was hot. We were far from any signs of civilisation. Where on earth was the Wise Man taking us?

He didn't give us time to think about that. He strode energetically to the bottom of the path. The Child and I hurried to catch up. I was panting when I reached the bottom. The Wise Man beamed.

He looked in the direction of the cliff and then gazed towards the desert.

'Which way?' he asked. Why on earth was he asking me? Didn't he know where we were going?

'I don't mind,' I shrugged.

'No, no. You decide.'

I hated making decisions. To me, crossing the road was a big decision, and making up my mind often took me days, even weeks of anguish.

'Where are we going?' I asked reasonably, hoping to forestall a decision.

'You decide.' His eyes were black and merciless.

I looked around. Great, I thought. It's a choice between a cliff and a desert. I was feeling desperate. 'I really don't mind. Whatever you think best.'

'What would you like to do?' he persisted.

'I don't know,' I said irritably because he was putting me on the spot. 'I don't care.'

'If you don't know and you don't care, why would you ever bother to move anywhere?'

'I don't often,' I said, feeling sorry for myself.

'I want to go up there.' The Child pointed at the cliff. Thanks a lot. Did he know I was scared of heights?

'I don't think we should climb a cliff. It could be dangerous.'

The Wise Man and the Child looked at me with what I thought seemed very close to contempt. So I was a coward, so what!

'Then you want to go into the desert?' asked the Wise Man.

No, I didn't want to go into the desert.

'Isn't it a bit hot to be walking in a desert?'

'Then you want the cliff?' said the Wise Man.

'Yes, yes,' said the Child excitedly.

'Shut up,' I said.

The Child's face crumpled. He ran over to the tree and sat down in the shade. He hunched over his knees, miserably.

'Now look what you've done,' said the Wise Man.

'I'm sorry,' I yelled. The Child ignored me.

'Telling him to shut up and go away isn't going to achieve anything. He'll always be there. He is part of you. You might as well accept him and make friends with him.'

Why did I get the feeling the Wise Man was amused by all this? I trudged over to the Child and sat under the tree with him.

'I'm sorry, I really am.'

'It was only a suggestion,' he sniffed. 'You'll never make a decision, so somebody has to. And then when I do, you tell me to shut up.'

'I'm sorry,' I said again, irritated at his tone. He was wise beyond his years and yet so young and vulnerable.

'So,' he looked up eagerly. 'We can go that way?' He was pointing to the cliff towering above us.

'I'm not sure.'

'How can I ever know what to do if you keep mucking me around.'

'All right, we'll go up the cliff,' I said angrily.

The Wise Man appeared by my side.

'You're sure about this?'

'Maybe it will be cooler than the desert,' I said hopefully.

'So you want to go up the cliff,' he persisted.

'Yes, I think so!' I felt pressured.

'And you're prepared to take the responsibility for your choice? You shouldn't make a choice just because someone else wants you to.'

'Well, he never makes a decision unless someone else pushes him into it,' said the Child cheekily. I wanted to hit him.

'We're going up the cliff,' I said angrily.

'So be it,' said the Wise Man. He waited. 'Go on, then.' He pushed me towards the cliff.

'Wait for me!' The Child ran after me. I took his hand and we walked towards the cliff.

I realised the Wise Man was still under the tree.

'Aren't you coming?' I asked, dismayed.

He smiled. 'I'll see you later.' I hesitated.

'Quick, quick. Go, go. On your way.' He waved at me peremptorily.

'But . . . ' I said.

His expression brooked no argument. I was already regretting that I'd come on this journey.

My heart sank as I followed the Child and we began to climb the cliff.

5

THE CLIFF ROSE ABOVE US, BLEAK AND UNINVITING. The Child ran merrily ahead, not at all afraid. I looked back to the Wise Man but he had done his usual trick and vanished.

I was angry. He'd browbeaten me into going along with him and the moment I'd agreed, he'd forced me to go off on my own.

And why did we have to climb the cliff? Was it to test my courage? Well, I could do without that test, thank you very much.

I thought of all the things I wished I'd said to him. I should have stood up to him. I was a coward. I was embarrassed at my indecision in front of him and the Child. How dare he force me to make a decision like that, anyway? And then leave me on my own! How dare he!

I went on in this grumpy mood for quite a while. What would we find when we reached the top of the cliff? Some mythical beast ready to devour us? I wouldn't be the least surprised. Maybe we wouldn't reach the top. At least I wouldn't. I'd probably fall off through sheer terror.

I'd worked myself up into such a state that I didn't notice the Child was now very far ahead.

'Don't go so fast,' I yelled. He stopped only for a second to look back and then ran on. I was moving very slowly as I picked my way carefully up the path, through boulders and rocks. I slipped on the gravel several times, scraping my knees and hands and cursing the Wise Man again.

The path grew increasingly steep. There was no shade and it was very hot. The sun was high in the sky and it grew hotter as we climbed. I could hardly see the Child. He'd become a tiny figure in the distance.

'Come back,' I yelled, but I doubted if he could hear me.

I looked down and the ground was far away. Despite the heat, I felt a chill. Why on earth was I doing this? What were we trying to prove, I thought again.

'You only have to wake up,' a voice whispered in my ear. I was sure it was the Wise Man and I whirled around but there was no one there. The voice had seemed so clear, as if he was next to me.

'I only have to wake up,' I repeated grimly, but something in me wanted to continue this journey. I had agreed to go on his travels with the Wise Man and he had asked me to write about them. I didn't like to go back on my word.

But as I climbed higher, I became afraid. Would I be able to get down again? The Child had disappeared completely. I hoped he was all right. I hadn't heard a scream, so I supposed he hadn't fallen off.

The path became very, very narrow as I neared the top. Now the valley was below me on either side. I didn't dare look down. I was dizzy with fear. My clothes were wet with perspiration and the sweat kept getting in my eyes.

At least, as we climbed higher, there was a breeze and it wasn't so hot. Yet I was still perspiring as I slipped and fell and grunted and swore, and climbed further up, holding onto rocks for dear life, desperately frightened I was going to slip and tumble off the cliff.

Suddenly the Child leapt out of nowhere and shouted 'Boo!' and I almost did fall off.

'Don't do that!' I yelled, aware of how foolish I must have looked as I jumped in fright and slipped back a few paces.

I scrambled up to him. He was grinning and looked excited and happy. The happiest he had been since we had met. A dear little boy loving every moment of this adventure. I couldn't be too angry with him.

'You're such a slowcoach,' he said impatiently. 'Come on. We're almost at the top. Isn't it wonderful! Look at the view.'

'Wonderful' I answered grumpily. I hadn't looked at the view for quite a while. I'd been too afraid to look down.

We had almost reached the top of the cliff. The Child smiled and held out his hand. With his encouragement I managed the last few steps. He pushed and pulled me onto the final ledge.

I lay on my stomach, panting and sweating, my eyes closed.

'Are we really there?' I whispered weakly.

'Open your eyes,' said the Child.

I sat up and opened my eyes. The view *was* wonderful.

The Child knelt beside me and held my hand. I felt oddly moved by this little person with his hand in mine. We sat in silence. We had no words for the beauty before us.

Behind us, the desert. In front of us, lush green valleys and mountains, as far as the eyes could see.

And in the distance . . .

'Is that a city?' I wondered.

'Probably.'

My eyes were on the glistening spires far away. I knew in my heart this was why I'd climbed the cliff. To get my first view of the Silver City, as it later came to be called.

'I really want to go there,' I murmured. And I realised as I said it that it would happen. I had an intuitive feeling that some day, somehow, I would visit the Silver City.

'Perhaps we will,' the Child said, echoing my thoughts. He squeezed my hand excitedly. 'Aren't you glad you came?'

'Yes,' I smiled, dreaming of the Silver City, 'oh, yes.'

The Child and I sat together in silence for quite a while until we realised it was growing dark. How long had we been climbing? It didn't seem so long since the sun had been high in the midday sky.

'What do we do now?' I asked.

'We go down the other side, of course.' He pointed to the path before us. 'It's not as steep. You should be able to do it easily,' he said kindly, as though talking to an old man.

'Oh, no, I think we should go back.'

But as it grew dark, I knew I didn't really want to go down the way we had come. It had been difficult enough climbing in the light.

'Perhaps we should sleep up here,' offered the Child. 'We could make a camp fire.'

'I don't know how to do that, do you?'

'No,' admitted the Child. 'But we could learn. There's always a first time.'

I didn't want to spend the night there. The thought of being eaten by some mountain lion didn't appeal to me.

'No, I don't think we should spend the night up here. Anyway, what about the Wise Man? He'll be waiting for us.'

'He'll find us again, don't worry.' The Child patted my knee as if I were the child. 'So, what do you want to do?' he asked, sounding like the Wise Man.

'Perhaps you're right. We should go down the other side, before it gets dark.' I tried to sound authoritative.

'You're sure?' The Child was not convinced.

'Yes! I'm sure! Come on!'

'Right. Let's go!' he shouted happily. He sprang to his feet and started making his way down.

'Wait for me,' I said.

The Child was right. It was easier getting down. This path was much less precarious. It didn't take us long to reach the bottom, just as the sun sank into the horizon.

And there was the Wise Man, sitting under a tree, waiting for us.

'You took your time,' he said.

6

'WHAT TOOK YOU SO LONG?' ASKED THE WISE MAN cheerily. I could have hit him. I controlled my anger as best I could. The Wise Man knew I was furious and took delight in baiting me. His eyes gleamed with merriment.

I sat down wearily, aching from head to foot. The Child wasn't tired. He was still running about, full of energy. I leant my head against the tree and closed my eyes, aware the Wise Man was watching me. I decided to ignore him.

'Are you going to stay here all night?' he asked.

'I don't know,' I replied irritably. 'This was all your idea.'

'But your choice.' I opened my eyes to see him grinning at me. 'You chose to climb the cliff.'

'And what did that achieve?' I bit back, and wished immediately that I hadn't said anything.

'You could have chosen to go through the desert.'

'Would that have been any better?' I couldn't help asking.

'Who knows,' he shrugged, but I felt that he did know. 'You didn't want to walk in the hot sun.'

'I had to walk in the hot sun to climb the cliff,' I said bitterly.

'Exactly.'

He grinned. I felt he was trying to make me say or do something but I wasn't sure what it was.

'Did I make the wrong choice?' I asked finally.

'There is never a wrong choice. Just results.'

'That's all right then.' I closed my eyes, feeling better.

'But you didn't really make a choice,' the Wise Man continued.

'What!' I leapt to my feet. Really, this man was too much.

'Did you?' He smiled. 'You couldn't decide, so you let the Child lead you.'

'There wasn't much to decide,' I said, defending myself. 'Walk through the hot desert or climb a cliff in the hot sun.'

'Would you like to go back through the desert and see?'

'No, thank you.' I sat down again and closed my eyes. 'At least I saw the city,' I said.

'What city?' the Wise Man asked innocently.

'I saw a city. It had silver spires. Is that why you wanted me to climb the cliff?'

'Me?' He shrugged helplessly. 'We don't ask you to do anything. We have no power over you.'

I sighed. I was sure he knew about the city. We could talk about that later. I was too tired to care. I desperately wanted to sleep.

'I'd really like to rest. Where are we going to spend the night?' I yawned.

'Wherever you like.'

'Don't do this to me!' I shouted. 'This trip was your idea. So you decide where we go!'

'Well . . . I don't know . . . ' he said, suddenly seeming very indecisive. 'We could stay here. But . . .'

'But what . . . ?'

'Who knows? There could be wild animals around, you know. It might not be safe.'

I felt sick. I couldn't face climbing the cliff again. 'We could go back over the cliff,' he said, as if reading my mind. I groaned. I was so tired, I thought I might burst into tears. Why on earth had I agreed to help this mad man?

The Child came to my rescue. 'I saw a cave halfway up. We could sleep there. That would be fun.'

'Isn't there a house somewhere?' I asked weakly. 'Don't you have any friends, Wise Man, who can help us?'

The Wise Man smiled gently.

'Why do you fear so much? What is there to fear?'

His words seemed to reach inside me and touch my heart. When he chose, his words could calm you in a second. And then you loved him.

'I'm sorry. So what should we do?'

'We'll go to the cave. If that's all right with you. Unless you have any better ideas?'

He knew I didn't. If I was hesitant about climbing up to the cave, I changed my mind when I heard the howl of a dog nearby. Here we were, alone in the desert, far from anywhere, and surrounded by wild animals. Really!

The Child led us up the path and across the side of the cliff to a cave. It didn't take long. I hadn't noticed a cave on the way down. I had to admit it was clever of the Child to discover it.

It was very dark inside but the Wise Man fished in his pockets and brought out matches and some small candles.

'You just happened to have those with you,' I laughed. He ignored this and lit the candles.

I looked around the cave. On the ground were three sleeping-bags, conveniently waiting for us. The Wise Man lit a fire from some wood and paper in a corner. Obviously, the cave had been lived in before. Was it his, I wondered and had he planned this?

I was starving. As though he'd read my mind again, the Wise Man pulled out from behind a boulder some sandwiches wrapped in cellophane.

'You've been here before,' I said.

He didn't answer. The Child and I devoured the sandwiches and the Wise Man poured us some water from a jug—again mysteriously produced from behind a rock. The water was pure and tasted like no other water I'd ever had. It was nectar.

'Not so quickly. And leave some for us,' chided the Wise Man. I blushed. I was so thirsty and had drunk so greedily. I handed the jug to the Child.

I yawned and felt I must lie down. I could barely keep awake but I didn't want to appear rude. The other two did not seem at all tired.

'Now we make notes,' said the Wise Man.

'Notes,' I groaned.

'For your book. That's what you're here for.' He handed me a note pad and pencil, again magically produced.

And so I wrote about the first day of my travels with the Wise Man.

7

I SLEPT SOUNDLY AND DIDN'T DREAM. WHEN I WOKE, the Wise Man and the Child had gone. Sun was streaming into the cave. I leapt from the sleeping-bag in panic, terrified they had left me behind.

I ran to the door of the cave and stopped, transfixed by the beauty of the morning. I looked at my watch but it wasn't working. I sensed it was early, about five or six o'clock. Much earlier than I was accustomed to rising.

The sky was a crystal blue and I could see for miles. And again, in the distance, I could see gleaming buildings. Was it the same city?

I stood in the entrance of the cave and breathed in the stillness of the morning. I was smiling and suddenly excited that I had begun these travels with the Wise Man.

He and the Child were down below by the trees. To my surprise, there was a horse standing with them. I didn't know much about horses but I guessed it was only young. A small white horse. The whitest horse I had ever seen. And very beautiful.

I ran down the slope to join them and patted the horse.

'Where did he come from?'

'It's a she. And she's mine,' said the Child. 'I've called her Aladdin.'

'Aladdin is a boy's name.'

'It doesn't matter,' he said firmly. 'That's what she's called.'

The horse had the most beautiful eyes; they changed colour in the light and they stared at me as she nuzzled my shoulder lovingly. For a moment they were as blue as the sky above. She was a dear animal.

'Hello, Aladdin,' I whispered.

She nuzzled me again, as though she already knew her name.

'Names are very important,' said the Wise Man. 'They can save you. They have great power.'

'Do I need to be saved?' I asked.

'Only from yourself,' he replied.

He always had an answer to everything, I thought darkly.

'You took your time getting up,' he said. 'We have to leave shortly. We've a long way to go, you know.'

'Where are we going?'

'I don't know,' he shrugged.

'Then why are we going? If you don't know?'

'You made the choice. Over the cliff, and on. So that's where we go.'

'It doesn't have to be my choice, surely?' I said, exasperated. 'You're the one who wanted me to come with you on your travels.'

'Would you like to go the other way?'

'No!'

'Good. We'll go this way. Come, come.'

'What about breakfast?' I asked hopefully.

'No time for breakfast. You should have got up earlier.'

He put the Child on the horse and began to lead it away.

'Well, really!' I muttered under my breath. I followed reluctantly. I took one last look at the cliff and wondered if I would be returning this way. Somehow I doubted it.

'So, where did Aladdin come from?' I asked again.

'She was waiting for us,' said the Child mysteriously, as if that was all I needed to know. Why did I bother to ask?

We walked along in silence, the only sound the clip-clop of Aladdin's hooves in the dust. The sun began to burn high in the sky.

'Would you like to ride?' asked the Wise Man.

'I've never ridden a horse,' I said.

'There's always a first time,' he replied.

'I'm allergic to animals. They give me hay fever.'

'Pshaw!' The Wise Man raised his eyes to heaven. As if on cue, Aladdin stopped and the Wise Man motioned the Child to get down. He did so reluctantly.

The Wise Man waited for me to get on. There was no saddle on the horse. I was sure I'd never manage to climb up. Certainly not with any dignity. I shook my head firmly.

'I don't really want to ride.'

'What is there to fear?' said the Wise Man. 'Come, come. Up, up. Quickly.'

He clapped his hands and I found myself struggling to get on. The Child laughed. Aladdin stood still, looking very bored. After several attempts, I slipped and fell.

I felt foolish.

'I really would rather not,' I said haughtily.

'Oh, would you rather,' the Wise Man said, mocking my tone.

The Child grinned, the Wise Man waited. I found myself trying again, this time pushed from behind by the Wise Man and the Child. I flushed with embarassment. I'd totally lost all dignity.

I was on! Aladdin galloped away and I held on to her neck for dear life.

'Stop her!' I yelled.

The Wise Man and the Child roared with laughter. Aladdin went faster and faster. Was it my imagination or did her feet hardly touch the ground?

I was terrified. Then it was as if she spoke to me. Somewhere in my mind, a shy, gentle voice said: 'Don't be frightened. It's easy. Enjoy.'

I slowly relaxed. I held on less tightly. The breeze was in my hair and I felt I was flying. It was exhilarating. I looked behind to see if the Wise Man and the Child were watching, but they were tiny figures in the distance.

'This is wonderful,' I yelled. 'Whee, I'm flying!'

To please me, Aladdin went faster. The landscape flew past in a blur. It was as if Aladdin and I were one.

Finally she wheeled around and took me back towards the Wise Man and the Child. She slowed and came to a halt. I got down unaided.

'That was wonderful!' I had a huge grin on my face. I put my arms around the horse and she nuzzled my cheek.

'Thank you, Aladdin.'

'Where's your hay fever?' asked the Wise Man.

'Do you know, that's amazing. I haven't got it. Perhaps I'm not allergic to Aladdin?'

'Perhaps you're not allergic,' he said darkly.

'I always have been before,' I shot back.

'You've been many things before and you will be many different things afterwards. It's your choice. If you want to be allergic, be allergic.'

'I didn't decide to be allergic to horses!' I said angrily.

'Didn't you?' he asked, looking through me with those piercing eyes of his. 'Anyway, now you can ride them, perhaps they won't make you sneeze.'

He always had the last word. The Child got back on Aladdin and we moved forward.

In the distance there was a dark cloud. Now there was a chill in the air. The sun was lost in a mist that was floating towards us.

I heard laughter. Loud and mirthless. It boomed through the air and surrounded us.

'What on earth is that?' I asked.

The Wise Man looked grim.

'There's a storm coming. We must find shelter.'

'But it's all flat around here,' I shouted through the awful laughter, 'there's no shelter anywhere near here.'

The laughter grew louder and a voice spoke. A deep, rolling voice. An unkind voice.

'That's right,' said the voice, 'there's no shelter.' It cackled mirthlessly.

'Who is that?' I asked again. The Wise Man didn't answer. Aladdin neighed and paced nervously.

Lightning flashed in the sky. It was very dark and the sun had disappeared completely. Loud thunder and more flashes of lightning. Aladdin neighed again in fear. The Child clung to her neck.

'I'm frightened,' he cried.

The lightning struck around our feet in nasty little

bolts, as if it was trying to hit us, and a savage wind lashed at us. The dust and mist swirled around us and soon I could barely see my friends.

The laughter roared in my ears, it seemed to be in my very soul. Then cruel hands began tearing at me from out of the darkness and I heard the weird shrieks of creatures, like bats, attacking me and clawing at my clothes.

'Help me, Wise Man,' I screamed.

I couldn't see where he was. I was in total blackness. I hit at the hands that clutched at me and covered my face in terror. I sank to my knees. Again the awful, mirthless laughter.

'Go back to where you came from,' said the voice.

'No!' I shouted.

'Then you will be sorry.'

The wind renewed its vigour, beating at me, and the hands clutched and scratched at me. I sank into the dust which swirled over me. I was sure I would be buried in it.

'Help, Wise Man. Help!' I screamed again.

A figure appeared out of the darkness and took hold of me. It was the Wise Man. He dragged me through the storm. It seemed, as he walked towards it, that it ran away from him. He held up an arm, still holding me with his other hand, and then there was silence.

The wind dropped, the mist cleared, the clouds dispersed. The sun reappeared. We were standing on the road.

Aladdin and the Child were safe, too, covered in dust, but alive.

'What *was* that?' I asked.

'The dark forces are always there to stop us reaching

the light,' the Wise Man answered enigmatically.

'Are we going towards the light?'

'I hope you are. If you're not, then you're going towards darkness.'

I do wish he'd give a straight answer to a simple question, I thought.

'But who was that man, the one who was laughing?'

'That's your enemy,' he said. 'He doesn't want you to come on this journey.'

'Why?' I asked.

'Because he doesn't want you to grow.'

He stared at me as though he could see a great darkness in me. He wasn't smiling.

'You still want to continue?'

I didn't stop to think. 'I said I would come with you, didn't I?'

He smiled mysteriously and I wondered why I was being so decisive all of a sudden. This trip wasn't turning out to be a lot of fun.

I knew the Wise Man was waiting for me to say something else.

'Shall we go on?' I said.

And so we did.

8

WE WALKED FOR HOURS. THE WISE MAN NEVER appeared to be tired. Nor did Aladdin, or the Child, who was excited by everything, especially the strange multi-coloured birds that often surrounded us and flew about the Wise Man's head. They would sit on his shoulder and chat to him. It was as if he could understand what they were saying. One even perched cheekily on Aladdin's head and rode part of the way with us, talking happily all the time. Gentle Aladdin was not at all bothered.

I became increasingly tired. I hadn't done so much walking in years. I'd never been interested in sport, or very good at it, and I was totally unfit. But I had been the one to say we should go on, and I didn't dare complain. I felt deeply resentful as we trudged further and further into the wilderness and my legs became heavier and heavier.

Finally I asked, as politely as I could, 'Do you think we could stop and rest for a while?'

'Of *course*.' The Wise Man was all largesse. 'I was wondering why you didn't ask before.'

We had come to another large cliff, towering above us, and the road led into a grove. We walked through the grove and found a beautiful little creek. We sat by the creek and drank the crystal-clear water. I watched Aladdin drinking thirstily and the Child playing in the water and I lay back on the grass and closed my eyes in relief.

'Now we can talk,' said the Wise Man.

I opened my eyes wearily. He was such a taskmaster.

'I *was* trying to rest,' I said with exaggerated politeness.

'Rest comes with food for the soul. The body must learn to obey the mind,' he said. 'When you fill your mind with light, then the body will be refreshed and co-operate with you.'

'And how do I do that?'

'If you listen, I'll tell you.'

So I sat up and tried to listen, though my eyes were heavy and I was desperate to sleep.

'Why do you think I asked you to come with me on these travels?' asked the Wise Man.

I hesitated. 'I'm not sure.'

'You think you're that special I should waste my time with you?'

'No. Of course not.'

Now that he'd asked, I was wondering why on earth I *was* putting myself through these exhausting adventures.

'You think I'm your Guru or something?'

'Are you?'

'Pshaw! We are nothing. How could we be a teacher to anyone?' If you think you can learn from me, you are wasting your time.'

'But you said you would give me food for the soul.'

'How can I give you what you already have?'

The man was too trying. I wished for once he would say what he meant without all this shilly-shallying.

'The food for your soul is within you,' said the Wise Man. 'No one can give it to you. You must find it for yourself. Go within and find it.'

'Then why am I coming on this trip with you?'

'That's what I was asking you.'

I closed my eyes. I'd had enough of his philosophy for one day.

'Don't go to sleep.'

I opened my eyes. 'Why not?' I snapped. 'I've walked for hours, I'm tired, I've agreed to go with you on this ridiculous trip and now you as much as tell me I needn't have bothered.'

'I didn't tell you to come.'

'You did. You said you'd been waiting for me.'

'Did I?' he asked innocently.

'And now you tell me I'm wasting my time.'

'Perhaps,' he said mysteriously.

I closed my eyes. I felt ridiculously close to tears. It was sheer tiredness, and irritation.

'Come, come.' He clapped his hands. 'You've had enough rest. We'll go.'

Enough rest! He hadn't stopped talking! For a moment I considered rebellion but I decided it wasn't worth the effort. I got slowly to my feet. I trudged along behind the horse and the Child, cursing the Wise Man.

He smiled at me.

'I enjoy our little chats,' he said. 'It's good to stretch the mind.' He winked. 'And the legs.'

Despite myself I grinned back. When he smiled, it was as if he had sent an arrow of light to your heart, and your spirits lifted. I realised I wasn't tired any more. There was a new spring in my step as I hurried to catch up with him.

'So why am I coming on this trip?'

'To find yourself,' he replied.

That gave me food for thought for at least another hour.

9

THE PATH WE WERE ON DISAPPEARED BETWEEN TWO giant cliffs. We entered into darkness. Huge sheer walls towered on both sides of us. Only the sound of our footsteps and Aladdin's hooves echoed in the eerie silence. Even the Child stopped chattering.

It was a long, lonely walk between the cliffs. The further we walked the darker it became, and there was only a tiny glimpse of blue sky above. How awful it would be to be trapped in such a desolate place. I pushed the thought from my mind. The Wise Man looked grim as he strode ahead. I sensed he was in a hurry to get us out of there.

Then we heard the laughter again. The deep, booming, cheerless laughter that struck fear into the depths of my soul. Rocks began to fall, narrowly missing us. Aladdin whinnied in terror.

'We must hurry,' said the Wise Man. 'We don't want to be trapped in here.' My stomach lurched. My worst fears were confirmed. We started to run.

We weren't allowed to run far. More and more rocks began tumbling, hitting the ground in front of us and behind us, until we were frightened to move. It was like the beginning of an avalanche.

'Quick!' yelled the Wise Man, and he dragged us forward into a crevice in the cliff. There we waited as the fall of rocks increased and the hideous laughter merged with the sound of the crashing rocks.

'Why does he want to hurt us, Wise Man?' My voice was quivering.

'He is my enemy. And yours. He has all the forces of darkness at his command.'

I swallowed nervously.

'Why is he my enemy? I haven't done anything.'

'He is every negative thought that mankind has ever had. He is a powerful energy created by you and everybody who ever allowed negativity to take control of their lives.'

'Then what can we do?' I asked.

'Stay calm, and reflect the light.'

Easier said than done. I was distinctly *uncalm* as the rocks whistled about my ears and the laughter filled my eardrums with painful noise.

The rocks began to pile up at the entrance of the crevice.

'We're going to be trapped in here,' I gasped.

Aladdin neighed and skittered back as far into the crevice as she could. The Child began to cry.

'We must get out!' I was panicking.

'SILENCE!' roared the Wise Man.

He held up his hands and the look in his eyes silenced us. He began to glow. His body filled with light. I could see all the veins and muscles as though in an x-ray.

The light flowed from his body and filled the crevice.

It grew until the Child and Aladdin were also glowing. I looked down and my own body was shining with the light.

The cloud of light drifted towards the entrance. The rocks that were piling up and barring our way, started to glow.

The evil laughter faded away and rocks stopped falling. I took a deep, calming breath. I was no longer afraid. We stepped over the rocks and back onto the path.

A little nervous whinny made us turn back. Aladdin couldn't step over the rocks. She neighed again and backed into the crevice.

'It's all right, Aladdin. Don't be frightened.' I went to help her.

To my amazement, Aladdin rose up in the light and floated through the air over the rocks and onto the path, where she landed with a proud little skittle, almost like a giggle. She looked at me as though to say: There! Beat that.

I was astonished. A flying horse! I'd only seen it in the movies. But then this adventure with the Wise Man was turning out to be better than any movie.

'Wow!' gasped the Child. 'Aladdin, how did you do that?'

But the Wise Man was impatiently pushing us towards Aladdin.

'Quick! Quick!' he shouted. 'There's no time to lose. Get on.'

I clambered up behind the Child onto the horse.

'Go,' yelled the Wise Man, and the horse rose up in the air and gently galloped towards the end of the cliffs.

'What about you?' I called. He didn't answer, just waved us on.

At that moment, the light in his body faded and he was barely visible because the rocks were falling again. Dust rose from the ground and hid him from our view.

'Wise Man!' I screamed.

The Child echoed, 'Wise Man!'

It was too late and we were too far away for him to hear our helpless screams.

Aladdin flew high into the air and through the narrow entrance between the two cliffs, as the rocks became an avalanche, falling onto the spot where the Wise Man stood.

10

As Aladdin flew out from between the cliffs and into the sunlight there was a resounding creaking noise behind us. I couldn't believe I was seeing it, but the two enormous cliffs were closing together.

'Get out, Wise Man. Get out!' screamed the Child.

Aladdin drifted to earth. We watched helplessly as the two cliff walls groaned and creaked towards each other.

'Wise Man!' I shouted. But I knew he couldn't hear me. We were too far away.

Then with an almighty groan the cliffs joined one another to form a mountain. An immense cloud of dust filled the air and, when it had settled, it was as though the two cliffs had never existed.

In the silence the Child was crying. I put my arm around him. Aladdin whimpered softly and laid her head against my chest, tears in her eyes. I wanted to cry myself but I held back. I patted Aladdin with one hand and stroked the Child with the other.

'Will he be all right?' asked the Child.

'I'm sure he will be.' I tried to sound more confident than I felt.

'Let's go and see!'

'But it's dangerous . . . '

'Please . . . ' the Child begged, his little face full of pain. Aladdin tugged at my sleeve with her teeth, pulling quite hard. She was telling me to get on her back. She obviously agreed with the Child.

She lifted up and flew us closer to the mountain. We landed softly in front of it. There was an awful silence about the place. We approached and, to our horror, couldn't find where the cliffs had joined together. All signs of the entrance had vanished.

'Wise Man, are you there?' the Child called, his little voice trembling.

There was no answer. We stood dejectedly in front of the mountain.

'I'm sure he's all right,' I said again. 'He's a Wise Man, isn't he? So he could do anything if he wanted to.'

Aladdin made a small sound of agreement and rose slightly off the ground.

'Did he teach you to fly, Aladdin?' I asked.

Aladdin nodded her head and flew a little higher.

'Then he could fly out of there,' said the Child hopefully. 'After all, he can make himself appear and disappear at will, can't he?'

'Of course he can,' I said.

'Then he'll be all right. He'll be safe!' His little face belied his words. My heart went out to him for his courage.

'He *will* be,' I said, and I meant it. I was determined to be brave, too.

At that moment, the laughter began. The voice boomed out.

'You think so, do you?'

The laughter shook the ground and stirred a breeze around us. The breeze became a wind which threatened to blow us off our feet.

'Run,' screamed the Child. He took my hand and we ran to Aladdin and hopped on her back. She struggled to rise in the air but the powerful wind blew her from side to side and she couldn't make any headway.

'Don't go yet. I want to talk to you,' ordered the voice, and laughed again. As if at his command, Aladdin sank to the ground and the wind stopped.

The Wise Man appeared.

'Wise Man!' we yelled joyfully. We leapt off the horse. As we approached him the Wise Man cackled evilly and we recoiled.

'You're not the Wise Man,' I said.

Then the booming voice came from the lips of the creature that appeared to be the Wise Man.

'I can be whatever you want me to be,' it laughed.

'Where's the Wise Man?' I said.

'He's gone. He can't help you now. But I will—if you'll let me.'

The voice now pleaded with us like a hurt child. The thing that was the Wise Man moved towards us, hands outstretched for help.

'Please help me. I'm so lonely.'

We started to back away but the voice was so persuasive we hesitated. The face of the Wise Man became kind and the eyes pleaded with us.

'Please . . . ' he said.

We stopped, not knowing what to do, and in that second's hesitation he had grabbed the Child and pulled him away by the hair, laughing again in that awful booming voice.

'No!' I yelled and hit at him. But every time I touched him I shrank back as sharp pains went through me like electric shocks and I had to let go. The mocking laughter filled the landscape.

'Help me!' the Child screamed.

I ran again at the man to try to pull the Child away. Again the electric shocks doubled me up with pain. I could see sparks flying from the man's body.

Aladdin gave a loud neigh. She rose in the air and galloped towards him. She flew around his head and kicked savagely at him with her hooves. He screeched and tried to defend himself and at that moment the Child was able to escape and run into my arms.

Aladdin turned and flew back to us. We leapt on her back and she carried us away.

'I'll get you for this,' yelled the man.

The wind began again but this time Aladdin was too high in the sky. It couldn't stop her. We sped into the clouds, away from the wind which shrieked at us . . .

'I'll get you! I'll get you!'

11

WE FLEW INTO THE SUN. ALADDIN SPED FASTER THAN before, as though she had wings, her long legs striding through the air. Perhaps she wanted to put as much distance as she could between us and the Evil One.

To think of him, chilled me to the bone. What had the Wise Man said? 'Every negative thought that mankind has ever had.' I shuddered. If that was what negative thoughts had created I would never be negative again.

But we had lost the Wise Man. That made me feel very negative. I wouldn't think about it now. I had to believe he would somehow survive the illusions created by the Evil One.

'You were very brave back there,' whispered the Child in my ear.

'Brave? I was as frightened as you.'

'But even though you were frightened you tried to save me. That was brave,' he replied solemnly. I turned to smile at him. His little eyes were very serious.

'Thank you,' he said. 'You really do care for me.'

'Of course I care for you!'

I realised I did care for this strange Inner Child who

was so much a part of me, and whom I had ignored all my life.

'We're a good team,' he said. 'When we work together.'

Was that a dig, I thought, for all the times I had ignored him. I smiled.

'We're a good team.'

He responded by hugging me tightly.

We sped on into the sun. Past valleys and deserts and many strange lands. It was a wonderful feeling to be sitting on Aladdin's back and flying. We weren't at all nervous. It was exhilarating.

Finally, I sensed Aladdin had begun to tire. She was pushing herself and her strides were no longer as fast and furious as before. I stroked her brow and whispered in her ear: 'I think you should rest, Aladdin.'

She nodded in agreement and slowly we sank back to earth. We landed on a hilltop, looking down into a small valley. We could see houses scattered around the hillside.

'At least people live here,' said the Child. It was a relief to know we had found human company at last.

Aladdin chewed hungrily on the grass. I stroked her back.

'Thank you, Aladdin. You have been so kind. You saved our lives.'

She nuzzled me, and her eyes, as they smiled at me, were deep purple.

From the position of the sun I could tell it was late afternoon. We must have flown for hours but it seemed like minutes.

'I'm hungry,' said the Child. We sat down on the

edge of the hill and contemplated the valley.

'When Aladdin's finished her grass, we'll go down.'

'Do you have any money?' he asked.

'No.'

'Oh well, we'll get some if we need it.'

'I hope so.' I sounded so negative. I thought of my resolution to change my negative thinking. 'Of course we will,' I added. 'And we may not need it. Some kind person might feed us. After all, this is an adventure, isn't it? And good things happen in adventures.'

The Child grinned, nodding excitedly. Then his face fell. 'Not always,' he said. 'We've lost the Wise Man.'

'Maybe we haven't. Maybe he'll turn up. Perhaps this is a test for us.' I didn't really believe my words.

'What kind of a test?'

'Maybe we have to believe he's all right. Like we believe we'll find money and food. If we really believe the Wise Man is safe, then he'll come back to us.'

The Child thought about this. 'After all, he disappeared at the start of our journey, didn't he?' he said.

'Yes, and he came back when we least expected it,' I pointed out eagerly.

'So he'll come back again?'

'He certainly will.' I found myself believing my own positivity.

We sat together for a few minutes, both feeling positive and happy at the thought of the Wise Man appearing as before.

'But what do we do now?' The Child's face was solemn again. 'Where do we go? We don't know what he wanted us to do. How do we go on without him?'

'We can't go back.' I replied. We certainly didn't want

to face the Evil One again, so there was nothing for it but to go on.

The Child agreed. 'We'll just hope the Wise Man appears when he's ready.' He held my hand. 'Why don't we think about him? He might be able to tell us where he is.'

He was no fool, this Child. We closed our eyes and tried to think of the Wise Man. I pictured him as I last saw him, standing in the light. Then I saw the cliffs closing in on him, and I shuddered.

In my thoughts, I shouted: 'Stop!' I tried to picture the cliffs opening again. It took a great deal of willpower. The memory of them closing was still so powerful in my mind. I struggled to change the picture. I managed to move the cliffs apart slightly but they started to close again.

'Run, Wise Man,' I yelled.

The Wise Man didn't move, only stared at me with a curious expression. As the cliffs moved to close in on him, I pushed them open again.

I was angry, and my anger gave me energy.

'You will open and stay open!' I commanded. The cliffs started to close. I said more confidently: 'No! You are open now.'

The more I said this with confidence, the easier it became. I really believed what I was saying and the cliffs started to open.

The Wise Man became full of light again. He was smiling at me. The light filled the cavern and with a loud bang the cliffs opened and stayed open.

Smiling, the Wise Man walked out into the sun.

I opened my eyes.

'You did it!' the Child said, amazed.

'Could you see?' I wondered how on earth he had read my mind.

'You pushed the cliffs apart. You saved him!'

'But it was only in my imagination,' I said. The Child was disappointed.

'Anything's possible!'

'Yes, it is!' We had power to do anything if we really tried. 'Come on,' I said. 'Let's imagine saving him again.'

We held hands and closed our eyes. Aladdin nudged my shoulder.

'Not now, Aladdin. We're concentrating.'

A voice behind us said: 'Don't overdo it.'

We whirled around to see the Wise Man standing there.

'Wise Man!' the Child exclaimed, laughing delightedly.

'Just a minute,' I cautioned, and held him back. 'How can we be sure it's really him?'

'Pshaw!' said the Wise Man, sounding very much like himself.

It was Aladdin who decided for us. She nuzzled the Wise Man with her nose and whimpered excitedly. Her eyes were the colour of gold. The Wise Man caressed her.

'It *is* you, Wise Man,' I said.

'Of course it's me. Who else would it be?' he replied, his eyes gleaming mysteriously.

'We saved you!' The child skipped around the Wise Man.

I couldn't help thinking that it was I who had saved the Wise Man but I let the Child have his moment. It didn't matter. The Wise Man was alive.

'Wise Man, we're so glad to see you,' I said.

'Yes, yes. I know,' the Wise Man answered. 'What are you standing around for? I thought you said you were hungry?'

Turning his back on us, he led us down a path into the valley. At least he could have thanked me, I thought miserably.

He turned back and looked at me directly, as though he had read my thoughts. His eyes were unfathomable. He winked at me. 'You're learning,' he said. Then he turned away and we followed him.

12

As we hurried down the path, I caught up with the Wise Man.

'I don't understand.'

'What?' he asked innocently.

'I thought we had lost you back there,' the Child chipped in. 'When those cliffs closed . . . Ugh! It was horrible.'

'So how did you get out?' I asked.

'You saw what happened,' the Wise Man replied. 'Do you need to ask questions?'

'I imagined . . . we imagined that we pushed the cliffs aside. It was creative visualisation, or something.'

'Pshaw!' The Wise Man was obviously not into such terms. 'You read too many books.'

'If I don't read, how do I learn?'

'By practice. Practise what you already know in your heart.'

That silenced me for a moment.

'But when we visualised . . . imagined that I . . . we . . . saved you, that was hours after we saw the cliffs close.'

'So?' The Wise Man was obviously growing impatient with my questions. 'Time is unimportant. Time in this world is not as you know it in your world. You place too much importance on time.'

And that was the end of our discussion.

It was evening when we came to a little weatherboard cottage with a pretty garden and a white fence around it. A scent of frangipani wafted on the air.

We left Aladdin outside. The Wise Man pushed me forward to knock at the front door.

'All right, all right. I'm coming,' said a voice from inside the house.

The door was flung open by a little old woman wearing a dark dress and a grey bonnet. Her clothes were of another age. Her skin was unlined and smooth and her eyes twinkled, even though she stood at the door in mock anger.

'You took your time,' she said in a gruff little voice. 'Well come in, if you're coming in.'

She bustled back into the house, expecting us to follow. When I hesitated the Wise Man gave me a shove.

'Go, go,' he said.

The old woman led us down a dark little hall into a roomy kitchen that looked onto a garden. In the distance we could see the hills, and the sun slowly sinking. The garden was full of vibrant coloured flowers, which gleamed in the fading light.

The kitchen table was set for four. The woman stirred a pot of soup on the stove. She motioned us to sit.

'Sit down then. It's all waiting for you. If you don't eat, the soup will be cold.'

How had she known we were coming? I glanced at the Wise Man but he didn't seem in the least surprised. So why should I be? I'd been with him long enough now to expect the unexpected.

The woman ladled out soup that smelled delicious. She gave us warm bread rolls and then stood with her hands on her hips, waiting for us to eat.

'Eat, then, eat.' She sounded exactly like the Wise Man. I wondered if they were related.

The Wise Man, reading my mind, said casually, 'Oh, this is my sister, Louise.'

Louise nodded, unsmiling, but her eyes twinkled.

'Hello, Louise,' said the Child as if he'd known her all his life. 'And Aladdin, our horse, is outside. Could we have some food for her?'

I felt guilty I hadn't thought about food for poor Aladdin, after she had saved our lives.

'We should give her some water, at least . . . ' I started to rise from the table but Louise pushed me down.

'I'll attend to the horse. Eat your soup. I don't want it to get cold,' she said crossly. She left the room to look after Aladdin.

'Eat, eat,' said the Wise Man, sounding just like Louise. I started to eat but was immediately stopped by the Wise Man.

'Dear God,' he prayed, 'we give thanks for this food.'

'Thank you, Lord,' piped the Child.

'Thank you,' I mumbled. I wasn't used to saying grace. I began to eat but again the Wise Man stopped me with his hand.

'Well?' He glared at me. I could read his mind.

'Er . . . and thank you for saving our lives.'

‘Good. Good,’ said the Wise Man, now eagerly gulping down his soup. ‘We need all the help we can get,’ he added with relish.

I almost choked on my soup.

13

THE CHILD AND I SLEPT IN A LITTLE ROOM UPSTAIRS IN The cottage, in single beds. The comforting scent of frangipani drifted through the open window.

After we had finished eating the Child was almost falling asleep at the table and I wasn't far behind.

'Go to sleep. Get some rest,' said the Wise Man.

'What about you?' I asked.

'Pshaw!' he said, as though he'd never heard the word sleep. 'Go, go!'

He waved his hand at me and I felt like a child myself.

I gently shook the Child awake and said to Louise, 'Goodnight, and thank you for dinner.' She smiled a crinkly smile. She sat in her armchair by the fire, knitting. She and the Wise Man had been talking in whispered tones all evening.

The Child and I followed Louise upstairs and she showed us to our room. I was asleep almost as soon as my head touched the pillow, the scent of the frangipani wafting on my breath. I smiled as I closed my eyes and heaved a happy sigh. It was wonderful to sink into a soft bed with clean crisp sheets.

But I fell into a dreadful nightmare.

I stood before the cliffs again. They had been pushed apart and I entered the path leading between them and into the darkness. I was alone. I heard the booming laughter of our enemy.

'Come in,' he said.

I was hypnotised and couldn't stop myself being drawn further into the darkness.

'Come along,' said the voice, now all sympathy and mock comforting. 'Come and be with me.' He roared with laughter and even though I was terribly afraid, my body continued to move forward.

I stood between the cliffs, in the awful darkness, terrified I was going to be trapped there and that the walls were going to close in on me, yet unable to move.

A giant shadow rose up in front of me. The dark wraith slowly assembled and took a human shape. Something in a black hooded robe towered over me. I couldn't see its face under the shadow of the cowl, only gleaming yellow eyes like a cat's—glistening in the dark, laughing slyly at me.

A long, thin hand pointed a sinewy finger from under its shrouds. A sharp, dirty fingernail beckoned to me.

'Come to me.'

I was shaking with fear. I wanted to turn and run but I couldn't. I found myself walking towards the dark figure, almost enjoying my powerlessness. Giving in to its mesmerising charm, even though I knew I shouldn't.

I walked closer and closer towards the beckoning hand. I knew in a second it would grab me and I would be lost, yet I no longer had any will of my own . . .

And then I awoke to find myself tossing and turning feverishly in my bed. A dark figure stood by the side of the bed. I almost screamed, until I realised it was the Wise Man.

'Ssh!' he whispered, and put his hand on my forehead, which was wet with perspiration.

'Ssh,' he said again gently. My breathing calmed and I drifted back to sleep.

This time I didn't dream terrible things. I was in a golden field with the Wise Man, the Child and Aladdin. We were surrounded by flowers and we walked happily along with the sun beaming down on us.

I awoke at dawn. The Child was still asleep. Outside, the fields were shining in the early morning sun. I dressed and crept downstairs.

The Wise Man was sitting in the chair by the fire, which had gone out. His eyes were closed but he sat very straight. I moved closer to him, not sure if he was asleep or meditating.

'Well,' he said, without opening his eyes.

'I'm sorry, Wise Man. I didn't mean to disturb you.'

'You didn't,' he said, still with eyes closed.

'Don't you sleep at all?'

He opened one eye.

'I can't afford to sleep. What would happen to you if I did?'

I remembered my nightmare. Had he saved me from the terror of that dark shape by waking me?

'I had a nightmare. You came and woke me up, didn't you?'

'I did more than wake you up. You'll have to be more careful.'

'I can't help what I dream.'

'Can't you?' was his enigmatic smile. He closed his eyes, signalling our conversation was over.

I tiptoed out through the kitchen to the back garden. There I found Louise sitting on the verandah, rocking back and forth in an old chair, her eyes on the rising sun. Didn't anyone sleep in this house?

'You're up early,' Louise said, without looking up.

'It's such a wonderful dawn.'

'Yes. Sit here and breathe it in,' she said. So I sat with her on the verandah and breathed in the dawn. Louise patted my hand, giving me a warm smile.

'I'll get breakfast soon. You'll need a good breakfast to give you strength for your travels.'

'Where are we going, did he say?'

'Oh, he never says,' she smiled. 'He never says when he's going or when he's coming.'

'Then how did you know to expect us, last night?'

Louise shrugged. 'I usually get a feeling. You don't need to be told things all the time, surely?'

No, I thought. I suppose I didn't. Sometimes you just knew things. I thought about my nightmare. Had it been a premonition? I was sure we weren't finished with the dark force that had tried to destroy us.

I shuddered involuntarily. Louise patted my hand again, as if she knew what I was thinking.

'Breathe in. Calm your nerves.'

I sat breathing in the dawn, trying to feel the joy of a new day—and to leave behind the nightmare that had haunted my dreams.

14

LOUISE PREPARED US A DELICIOUS BREAKFAST. THE Child wouldn't eat until he was sure Aladdin had been fed. What a kind child he was! I was guilty again that I hadn't thought about Aladdin. I'd been too selfishly enjoying breakfast.

The Wise Man was very quiet. He didn't answer any questions, except with a grunt or a snort, which made me feel I'd been idiotic to ask them. After a while his dark mood affected us all and breakfast was finished in silence. I wondered what he was brooding over but I didn't dare ask.

We were finishing our cups of tea when he suddenly said: 'Come, come—don't dawdle. We have a long way to go today.' I leapt to my feet. He always managed to take me by surprise.

'Where are we going?' the Child chirped.

'Who knows?' the Wise Man shrugged.

'How can we get there if we don't know where we're going?' I asked, exasperated.

'You decide.' The Wise Man smiled sweetly at me.

'That's not fair!'

'You want me to decide—is that fair? Then if I take you on a hard path, you'll complain and blame me.'

'But it was your idea to go on this trip. I've just come along.'

'Ah!' The Wise Man pointed a finger at me. 'So! If you wanted to come along, you must want to go somewhere.'

'Well, yes,' I said reluctantly. 'I don't want to climb any more cliffs.'

'Pshaw! You managed that all right.'

'You did!' the Child joined in.

'I did, didn't I?' I answered proudly.

'It wasn't so bad,' said the Child. 'I enjoyed it, really.'

'So,' said the Wise Man, 'where do you want to go?'

'Let me choose,' said the Child. The Wise Man waited.

'No,' I said. They both looked at me.

'You choose, Wise Man,' I begged.

'Pshaw!' The Wise Man raised his eyes to heaven and motioned us to follow him.

Outside, Aladdin was waiting impatiently at the gate, delighted to see us. She nuzzled me happily, pushing her gentle face into my shoulder.

We thanked Louise, who was sad to see us go. She handed me a brown paper bag full of delicious sandwiches for our lunch.

'Be careful,' she said. 'Go on a straight path.'

We set off, continuing the way we had come—along the edge of the valley. I looked back to wave to Louise but she had gone. Indeed, the little house had gone. I looked in amazement, but now there was only greenery where I was sure the house had been. I decided not to say anything. In the Wise Man's company anything was possible.

The Wise Man looked at me.

'There are three things you must learn, if we are to succeed in our mission.' He smiled mysteriously.

'Yes?' I swallowed nervously. His eyes were dark and he was looking at me again as though he could see into my soul and didn't like what he saw.

'Yes?' I said again.

'You must try not to fear. Learn to trust and believe in yourself. Your true self. The self that belongs to God.'

'So what are the three things?' I asked.

'Dummy!' he yelled. 'I just told you. Don't fear. Trust. And believe.'

'I understand.' I wondered if I did.

'Don't fear. Trust. And believe,' the Child marched along to the words, kicking out his sturdy little legs. He made it into a chant.

The Wise Man was still looking at me.

'I'll try,' I said.

'Good.' He smiled a wicked smile. We had come to the end of the path. Down below us were further valleys and in the distance the glistening spires of the city. Or what I believed might be a city.

The Wise Man stopped.

'So. You choose.' I hated him for that.

'Must I?'

'Don't fear,' he said.

They were all waiting. Aladdin, the Child and the Wise Man. I had the old familiar sinking feeling in my stomach. I couldn't make this decision! I didn't want to! Why was he doing this to me!

I wanted the ground to swallow me up. Anything to escape this moment. They were still waiting. I looked around desperately.

'Is that a city?' I asked. 'Those spires in the distance?'

'Yes,' said the Wise Man.

'Very well. I want to go there.'

Anything to make a decision. Anyway, I did want to go to the city. At least I thought I did.

The Wise Man looked sad as though I had failed the test.

'Really? You're sure you want to go there?'

My heart sank. 'Yes. I think so.' I didn't sound so convincing.

'It's such a long way,' said the Wise Man, suddenly all concern for my welfare.

'Oh well.' I was easily persuaded. 'Where would you like to go?'

'Dumbbell!' yelled the Wise Man. 'Trust yourself. If you want to go to the city, go! Trust your own judgement.'

'All right,' I said, not at all firmly. 'We'll go.'

'You're sure?' The Wise Man looked doubtful again. I wasn't going to be taken in.

'I'm *sure*!' I said, feeling a new-found strength.

'Good!' He patted me on the back. 'Goodbye. See you there.'

'Don't you want to go?' I asked, surprised.

'No, I've been there.'

'Then we'll go somewhere else.'

'Why? Are you afraid to go by yourself?' he asked.

I knew I was afraid, deeply afraid.

'Don't fear. Trust. And believe.'

And he was gone. Just like that. I was very angry. He got us into this, we saved his life, and now he'd left us alone again. Anything could happen.

'Don't fear. Trust. And believe,' sang the Child. He wasn't at all afraid. He saw the gloom on my face and took my hand reassuringly.

'He'll come back. He's just testing.'

I smiled, despite myself. The Child was much braver than I. Was this another test of the Wise Man's? Don't fear. Trust. And believe. I sighed. Only a little while ago I had decided not to be negative. Being positive was harder than I thought.

'You're right. He's just testing. Let's go.'

'To the city!' shouted the Child.

'I know. We'll fly,' I said, 'it'll be quicker, eh, Aladdin?' Aladdin didn't seem to hear. She stared straight ahead. We got on her back.

'Fly, Aladdin,' I urged. She didn't move. I leant forward and whispered in her ear. 'Fly, Aladdin.' She ignored me.

'What's the matter with her?' said the Child.

No amount of cajoling, or bullying, or shouting worked. She wouldn't fly. We got off.

'Do we walk, Aladdin?' I asked irritably. Aladdin nodded and trotted happily down towards the next valley. I looked at the Child. He shrugged.

'Life wasn't meant to be easy,' I said.

'Oh yes. It was! This is fun!' he yelled, and ran after Aladdin.

I said to the empty air: 'Thanks a lot, Wise Man.'

15

WE MOVED FURTHER INTO THE LOWER VALLEY. THE landscape became greener and very lush. It was a green the like of which I'd never seen. So bright I felt I was in an old Hollywood technicolour movie.

The beauty of the landscape calmed me. As we walked through the valley I wasn't so afraid. Soon the Child and I were laughing. Aladdin did a few little skips around us, sharing our enjoyment.

We came to a medieval village. There was one main cobbled street with tiny quaint houses on either side and narrow streets winding up between the houses. It was very quiet in the early morning sun but as we approached the first house, its doors opened and a family appeared: two children and a mother and a father. They smiled and waved as though they knew us.

'We're on our way to the city with the silver spires. Is it very far?' I asked. The man beamed and shook my hand effusively.

'Bring back the gold,' he said.

I wondered what on earth he was talking about.

'Thank you,' said his wife.

'Hooray!' shouted the children and danced around my legs.

'I don't understand . . .' I began, but doors started opening in every house along the street. People appeared from everywhere and began cheering. The Child and I stared at each other. We had no idea what we'd done.

We continued walking, with people cheering us as if we were royalty. Through the cheers I was aware of them chanting: 'Bring back the gold. Bring back the gold.'

I didn't know what on earth they meant. I was sure they had mistaken me for someone else. As we reached the end of the street a very old man sat on a bench.

'Excuse me,' I asked him, 'can you tell me the way to the city with the silver spires?'

'That is for you to find,' he replied enigmatically.

'Are we going the right way?' I asked.

'You will know when you are on the right path. Nobody goes to the Silver City uninvited,' he said.

So that distant place was called the Silver City. I turned towards the cheering crowd.

'Who are those people? Why are they cheering?'

'They hope you will reach the city and save them. You are their hope.'

'Save them? Save them from what? How could I save them?' I was totally bewildered and beginning to be afraid.

'We are all lost souls,' said the man. 'Only you can save us.'

I was speechless. The man watched me. Something about him seemed familiar. I felt I'd met him before, but then I couldn't have.

'What is the "gold"?' I asked.

'It is what we have lost. The light of our souls. And you will find it for us.'

'I can't do that!' I was angry and frightened. There must be some mistake. I didn't know these people. I'd never seen them before. Why should I be responsible for their souls? Once again I cursed the Wise Man for bringing me here—for making me decide to visit the city with the silver spires. I had obviously made the wrong decision.

'Only you can do it,' said the man. 'You are chosen. Do not fail us. We rely on you.'

The cheering had stopped and the people crowded around us. They watched silently as I talked with the old man. A few of them reached out to touch me. I pulled away.

'Let's leave,' I whispered to the Child. He nodded agreement. He was as puzzled as I was.

'What is this place?' I asked a final question of the old man.

'It is the Village in the Valley of the Lost Souls,' he said, as though it was the most normal thing in the world.

'How can they be lost souls, they look so happy.'

'They are happy because you are here. You will save them from the darkness.'

'I can't save anyone,' I said sharply. 'What are you talking about? What is wrong with them? They live in this beautiful place, it's lush and green . . . '

'It is only like that because you are here. It is how they would like it to be. And you are as they want you to be.'

'Look!' The Child pointed to my body. It was radiant with golden light. So was his, and Aladdin's.

She drifted above the ground, her body glowing. The crowd gasped in awe.

'They've given you all their good thoughts so you can save them,' said the old man.

'Save them from what?' I asked.

'From him. It is very different here when the Evil One comes.'

I didn't need to ask who he was talking about. It was our old enemy. I felt it in my bones.

'I can't save them from *him*!' Fear made my voice crack. 'He is too powerful.'

At that moment clouds formed in the sky. The sun disappeared. A rumble of thunder. I looked down and the light had gone from my body. The Child and Aladdin had lost their light. The crowd drew back in fear. They ran to their houses.

A howling wind sprang up. The old man rose from his chair.

'Don't fail us.'

Those were his final words before he disappeared into the house behind. It began to pour. The sky was black.

'We've got to get out of here.' I took the Child's hand and we started to run. We could hardly see the street in front of us. As we tried to leave, a savage wind pushed us back. We tried again. It was impossible to push through the wall of wind and rain.

We stumbled blindly to a house, leading Aladdin behind us. There the three of us huddled together under a balcony.

The dreadful laughter started, joining in with the rage of the storm.

'Ha, ha, ha! So you're going to *save* them, are you?' mocked the voice.

'Please! We don't mean you any harm. We just want to go on our way.' I was very frightened.

'You couldn't even save yourself, you weakling,' said the voice. The storm battered us furiously, almost blowing us off our feet. I put one arm tightly around the Child for fear he'd be blown away. Aladdin whimpered but stood her ground, her head down, desperately trying to stop herself being blown over.

'You fool!' shouted the voice. A crash of lightning burned near us, lighting up the darkness. The village looked like a harsh lunar landscape. The Child and Aladdin trembled.

'Please. Leave us alone,' I begged, my voice shaking. Another loud spurt of lightning danced around our feet. I was terrified. I knew we were going to be killed.

'You're nothing but a poor weakling,' the voice laughed. 'Who are you to think you can save anyone?'

'I really don't want to,' I said plaintively. 'We just want to go on our way to the Silver City.'

'You'll never find it,' said the voice. 'You haven't the will-power, or the strength or the courage.'

The lightning leapt at me and singed my hair. It was being thrown at me in darts, deliberately just missing me. But for how long?

'We will find the city,' shouted the Child bravely. 'And you can't stop us.' I could have hit him. I admired his courage but was afraid it might get us killed.

There was another roar of thunder and a crash of lightning.

'Can't I?' said the voice. The Child screamed in pain.

He was lit up by the lightning and he jumped around as it sent shocks to his poor little body.

'Stop it,' I cried out.

'You puny little person,' the voice laughed at me.

Aladdin pulled at my sleeve. At first I thought she wanted protection but she was dragging at me furiously. She rose a few steps in the air. She wanted to fly.

'Quickly!' I pulled the Child towards Aladdin. The wind tried to throw us back but I managed to hold the Child on and drag myself up behind.

I don't know how Aladdin managed, but she rose up through the wind and out over the street. The wind threw us from side to side but Aladdin, her every muscle straining, forced herself to fly higher into the storm until we had risen over the town.

The lightning whipped around us and the wind howled but Aladdin pushed through. Now she had found her stride and she leapt into the wind.

'Ha, ha!' said the voice. 'I'll let you go this time.'

'You'll never get us,' shrieked the Child. Aladdin neighed her agreement. She was flying at great speed now and we were leaving the storm behind.

'No. You won't get us!' I was filled with power and I really believed what I'd said. 'We will get to the Silver City and save the lost souls!'

At that moment I felt stronger than I'd ever felt before. My courage gave Aladdin more strength. We surged into the sky and in a moment we had left the storm behind. Suddenly we were above open fields and the sun was shining. There was no sign of the village. In the distance behind us was a dark cloud—and the faraway sound of thunder.

'Thank you, Aladdin,' I whispered. Aladdin nodded her head. She floated gently to earth.

We landed by a river, near a clump of trees. It was so green and peaceful that it was hard to believe we had just been through such a terrible storm.

Aladdin sank to her knees, exhausted. As we jumped off her back she groaned and rolled over on her side. Foam was hanging from her mouth.

'Aladdin? What is it? What's wrong?'

She lay with her eyes closed, hardly breathing. The strain of flying through the storm had been too much for her. By trying to save us she had used up all her strength.

'Oh, Aladdin,' screamed the Child. 'Please don't die!'

He looked helplessly at me. I didn't know what to do. I ran to the river and soaked my handkerchief with water. Then I squeezed the water into Aladdin's mouth. I wiped her forehead with the wet handkerchief. She opened her soft eyes and stared at me. They were a pale, pale blue. She closed them again. Her breathing was very shallow.

'Please don't die!' I repeated. We knelt on either side and stroked her gently. She hardly moved. Tears welled in my eyes.

'What are we going to do?' said the Child.

'She'll be all right,' I said, with more conviction than I felt. I turned away so the Child wouldn't see my tears. His own eyes were full of tears and they ran down his cheeks.

'Oh, Aladdin,' he whispered brokenly and threw his arms around her neck. Aladdin whimpered softly. I closed my eyes and prayed.

And then I remembered saving the Wise Man.

‘Remember how we saved the Wise Man? Do you think we can do it again?’

‘We have to try!’

So we sat together next to Aladdin. We put our hands on her poor, tired body and closed our eyes. And we tried to save her.

16

WE PICTURED ALADDIN FLYING THROUGH THE STORM, easily and effortlessly. Not the way it had been, but this time in control. She wasn't taxed by the journey but reached the ground relaxed and happy.

We concentrated on the picture for minutes. When we opened our eyes, Aladdin was as still as death. Her breathing came in tiny, exhausted spurts. Her eyes were closed.

'It's not working,' cried the Child desperately.

'It worked before! It must work!'

I clenched my eyes shut and forced myself to see Aladdin sailing through the terrible storm in full control, undisturbed by her efforts.

I tried too hard. My stomach was a tight knot of fear. The more I willed Aladdin to get better, the less confident I was. Now I was fighting my own fear. I opened my eyes. There was no change in Aladdin.

I closed my eyes again.

'Dear God,' I prayed, 'help me to help Aladdin. Don't let her die.' I tried to be calm. I took deep breaths. At first I didn't think it would work because I was so afraid.

But the courageous little Child sitting next to me, concentrating fiercely, gave me strength.

My breathing became more regular. I thought: I'm trying too hard. I must let go. I tried to let go of all my fearful thoughts. I remembered how, in the village, I had been filled with light.

As soon as I pictured the light I felt it surge through me. I opened my eyes to see my body glowing. I smiled. A deep calm touched my soul. The light flowed to the Child and together we were an enormous ball of light. The light spread through Aladdin's poor, tired body and it encompassed the three of us.

I could feel the warmth of Aladdin's body under my hand and I visualised the light healing every cell, every nerve, every tissue. I was confidently and joyously sure she would be healed.

I floated away into the light where there was no thought, no body. I was one with the universe, one with the beautiful light that filled all things.

I was beaming. My body began to quiver. I don't know how long I remained in that joyous state, but finally a voice whispered in my ear: 'It is done.'

The Child and I opened our eyes at the same time.

'She's better, isn't she?' the Child grinned. I looked around. Aladdin had gone.

'Aladdin, where are you?' There was an excited little whimper above my head. Aladdin was prancing in the air. She was healed.

'Hooray!' laughed the Child.

Aladdin jumped to the ground. She nuzzled us both in thanks. I put my arms around her.

'You did it,' said the Child.

'*We* did it!' Thank you, Lord, I whispered. Aladdin neighed and trotted down to the water where she drank noisily.

'Let's go for a swim,' shouted the Child. We threw off our clothes and scampered into the water. Aladdin joined us and we swam and played happily for hours.

Afterwards, we lay on the grass and ate the sandwiches Louise had given us for lunch. As we lay there, it was as if we hadn't a care in the world. I was happy just to have this moment and not think of the future.

'Did you mean what you said back there?' asked the Child.

'What did I say?' I hedged, knowing full well what he was leading to.

'That you would go to the Silver City, and save the lost souls.'

I couldn't meet his eyes. They made me uneasy.

'I don't know,' I replied at last. Then defensively, 'How could I save them?'

'We'd help you. Aladdin and I.' Once more I had to admire the Child's bravery.

'I don't know. We'll see.'

I chewed my sandwich and stared at the water, very aware the Child was watching me.

'You didn't mean it,' he said finally.

'I did. At the time.'

'You shouldn't say things you don't mean.'

'Look. I'll think about it. Okay?' I said, getting angry now.

'You're always *thinking* about things. But you don't often *do* much.'

'That's not true!' I coloured angrily. 'I saved the Wise Man and Aladdin.'

'With my help.' What an odious child.

We sat in silence. I didn't want to talk to him any more. His accusing stare made me uncomfortable. I walked to the water's edge.

I felt as if a heavy black cloud had descended on me. I could hardly breathe. My stomach quivered, I was nervous, I was angry, I wanted to run away. And yet I knew I couldn't.

There was a nuzzle at my shoulder. Aladdin's limpid eyes gazed into my face. I sensed she knew what I was going through. I hugged her.

'What am I going to do, Aladdin?' I laid my face against hers, her warm breath on mine. 'How can I help those people? I can't help myself most of the time.'

Aladdin looked at me as though she really didn't believe me.

'Why me, Aladdin? Why me?' I asked.

I was being severely tested. Where was the Wise Man when I needed him? Yet I was sure he was deliberately putting me through this. I was on my own.

I had been chosen, the old man said. Me! *Chosen*! What rubbish. I didn't *owe* these people anything. I didn't have to help them.

And how could I help them? Even if I managed to get to the city, what did I do then? Bring back the gold? What on earth did that mean? Save the lost souls! What a lot of poppycock! Somehow I knew it wasn't.

I sat by the river for a long time, feeling heavier and heavier, as if a dark blanket had wrapped itself around my soul. My thoughts turned in endless circles and I put myself through misery. And I really didn't have to, because deep in my heart I knew I was going to do what I had to do.

A little hand stole into mine. The Child fixed his large eyes steadily on me.

'Well? Are we going on?'

'Oh, I don't know,' I said irritably.

'Then do we go back?'

'I don't know that either.'

'Then what do you know?'

'Not much,' I laughed ruefully.

'Yes, you do! You're very strong. You helped save the Wise Man and Aladdin. You've fought off the darkness twice. You can do it again.'

Aladdin nuzzled agreement from my other side.

'But we don't know what we'll be getting into.'

'We haven't from the beginning,' said the wise Child. He always astounded me with his courage.

'You want to go on and save these people? However we're supposed to do that?'

'The Wise Man will help us. Don't you remember what he said?' The Child marched around me, chanting: 'Don't fear. Trust. And believe.'

Aladdin whinnied and cantered around with him. I joined in and we circled each other in a wild dance. 'Don't fear. Trust. And believe.' I laughed. My spirits lifted. For a moment I forgot my fears. We repeated the words over and over.

'Look!' The Child pointed at my body. It was radiant with light. As was his and Aladdin's.

'You can do it!' And I knew I could. I sank to my knees. The Child knelt with me.

'I can do it,' I whispered. 'I *will* do it. I will do what I have to do.'

'You solemnly promise?' demanded the Child. I looked at him. 'You can't break a promise.'

I took a deep breath.

'I solemnly promise . . . well, I'll try,' I said, getting feeble again.

'No, no, just promise. Yes or no,' said the voice of the Wise Man. We looked up and saw the old man from the township limping towards us.

'It was you all the time,' I shouted.

The old man melted before our eyes. In his place stood the Wise Man, grinning happily.

'Sometimes you need a little push,' he said.

'I knew you were around. I felt it,' said the Child.

I was angry again. I was being manipulated!

The Wise Man patted my cheek, his eyes twinkling.

'Don't worry. God never asks you to do anything you're not capable of.'

'Thanks a lot,' I said sulkily.

'So,' said the Child. 'What do we do now, Wise Man?'

'Well. I'll tell you,' said the Wise Man.

17

'WE HAVE TO BE VERY CLEVER TO GET TO THE SILVER City,' said the Wise Man.

'And what do we do when we get there?' I asked.

'Worry about that when you arrive. First you have to get there—and it won't be easy.' He eyed me compassionately. 'You're sure you want to go through with this?'

He was playing games again.

'No, I'm not sure,' I responded irritably. 'But now I've made a promise. And I always try to keep my promises.'

'Good man.' He again looked deeply compassionate.

'Don't feel badly if you fail. There's no shame if you don't get to the Silver City. Only a few ever find the way.'

'Have you been there?' piped the Child.

'It's so long ago. I've almost forgotten.'

'You must remember, surely?' I was annoyed by his flippant manner. He stared at me for a long minute.

'The way to the Silver City changes for each person. And when you leave, providing you finally get there, you may not remember *how* you got there. It could be removed from your mind.'

The Child and I were fascinated.

The Wise Man laughed.

'Well, if you did remember,' he said, 'you probably couldn't resist telling someone and then everybody would get there. And that's not the point of the exercise.'

'What is the point then?' I asked.

'Getting there is half the fun,' smiled the Wise Man.

'Let's go now,' said the Child excitedly.

The Wise Man paused. 'But first,' he said thoughtfully, 'you have to pass through the Valley of the Mirage, and very few people ever get through that successfully.'

I looked at him nervously. 'What happens if they don't get through?'

'Oh, they stay trapped there,' he said, with relish. 'But don't worry,' he added, seeing the expression on my face, 'in the Valley of the Mirage you have everything you want, if you want it. That's why it's so hard to leave.'

'Oh,' I said.

'What will get you through is remembering your quest and not being deceived by the mirage, because everything in the valley is unreal. Once you realise that, the mirage disappears. But very few people have the strength to see past the illusion. Do you think you can do it?' he asked eagerly.

I didn't know what to say.

'What sort of mirages are there?' I asked flatly.

'Whatever you want, whatever tempts you, it's all there.' He paused. 'Whatever you'd sell your soul for.'

I was distinctly uneasy.

'I don't know if I'll have the strength.'

'Pshaw! There you go again. Always doubting yourself. Haven't you learnt anything yet?'

'All right. I will have the strength—I will get through the Valley of the Mirage.'

'I hope so,' he said simply. Really, the man was impossible. You could never win.

'What happens *after* we get through the Valley of the Mirage?' I asked pointedly.

The Wise Man shrugged—one of his 'how could I possibly know anything' shrugs—'The way will be shown to you,' he said enigmatically.

'And are you coming with us this time?' I asked, fully expecting him to disappear again.

'I thought you'd never ask,' he said gleefully.

'Hooray!' said the Child. I was hugely relieved. If the Wise Man was to be our guide, nothing too bad could happen to us, could it?

But then I remembered the dark face of our enemy, and I wondered.

18

So we began the journey to the Valley of the Mirage. As we marched along the Wise Man gave me a warning.

'You must prepare yourself so that you are strong enough to get through the valley.'

'How do I do that?'

'If you'll listen, I'll tell you,' he snapped. So I listened.

It appeared that many people had tried to get through the Valley of the Mirage. Mostly they had failed. This cheered me enormously!

'You see, the valley was once a happy place, a Garden of Eden, and many of God's chosen people lived there,' said the Wise Man. 'It was a great spiritual centre and people came from far and wide to study there.'

'I've never heard of it before.'

'It was long before your time, dummy! I'm talking thousands of years ago.'

I wondered how he knew so much about it.

'The people developed the power of thought and learned the secret of the ages—that the mind creates everything.'

'Does it?' I asked.

'You've had some experience of that recently, haven't you?'

The Child and I had certainly used the power of our minds to rescue the Wise Man and bring Aladdin back to health.

'So, these people became very great at using the power of the mind, but they became very smug about it.' The Wise Man looked at me as though he suspected I might have become a little smug, having saved him and Aladdin. I blushed, because I had been feeling quite pleased with myself.

'And then they forgot who they were. That the power comes from God. We are all part of God, but these poor people in the Valley of the Mirage began to believe they were all-powerful and could do anything they wanted.'

He looked very grim as he told this story. I began to feel distinctly uncomfortable.

'So when they forgot who they were, they also forgot that they were creating illusions, and so they became fixed in whatever illusion they had created. The illusion became greater than them, and they were lost. And now they wander in illusion forever.'

'Like the lost souls I'm supposed to save?'

'Pshaw! Who are *you* to think you can save even one soul?'

'You told me that was what I had to do!'

'First things first—let's just get you through the Valley of the Mirage.'

'How am I going to get through if all others have failed?' My voice sounded very high pitched.

He shrugged: 'I don't know.'

'Oh, thanks.' Now I really was depressed.

The Wise Man smiled and patted my cheek. 'Don't fear. Trust. And believe.'

'We'll do it,' said the Child, taking my hand. I didn't feel so confident.

'All you have to do,' said the Wise Man, 'is see past the illusions—remember it's all an illusion and you can change it with your thoughts. It's easy.'

He winked at me, and I smiled despite myself.

'It's easy,' shouted the Child gleefully and he and Aladdin did a few little dance steps together, Aladdin cheekily swishing me with her tail. I grinned at them all.

'It's easy,' I shouted. 'It's easy.'

'Don't fear. Trust. And believe,' sang the Child.

We joined hands and skipped along, singing. There was a rumble of thunder. The sun disappeared behind some clouds. It was going to rain.

'Look, over there!' The Child pointed to a barn nestling among some trees. We ran to it as a small shower started. We pushed the doors open, and collapsed on a bale of hay, to catch our breath.

'Where's the Wise Man?' asked the Child.

I went to the doors of the barn and looked out. The sudden shower had stopped almost as soon as it had begun, and the sun was shining again. There was no sign of the Wise Man.

'Wise Man,' I called. 'Are you there?'

But no. He'd left us.

'We're on our own again,' I said turning back to Aladdin and the Child, who looked slightly fearful.

'He said it was easy.'

I wasn't so sure.

19

'EVERYTHING IS DIFFERENT,' EXCLAIMED THE CHILD, AS we left the barn and walked out into the sun. And it was. The path had disappeared and now there were long rows of trees, and houses on a hill where before there had been a valley. The houses were all very grand and beautiful.

We stood in amazement.

'Oh dear,' said the Child. 'Are you thinking what I'm thinking?'

I looked at him curiously. He was one step ahead of me.

'We're in the Valley of the Mirage.'

I looked again. 'This can't be a mirage, surely?'

'How did it get here, then? It wasn't here a moment ago.'

So this was the Valley of the Mirage.

'It's very beautiful,' I murmured.

'We've got to get out of here. Quickly,' said the Child.

'Don't panic!' I snapped. 'We will. If it's a mirage, we can just walk through it, can't we?'

The Child looked disbelieving.

'Now, let's see,' I pointed in front of me. 'We ran to the barn from over there—so we'll go back to where the path was and just keep walking in the direction of the city until we've left the valley.'

'How will we know when we've left, if it's all a trick?'

'We'll *know.* I don't know how we'll know, but we will.' We walked through the trees towards where we thought the path was. Aladdin kept stopping to eat the grass.

'Aladdin, come on. Don't delay. We're in danger,' said the Child.

Aladdin ignored us. The grass was obviously delicious.

'Aladdin! Come on, please,' I begged.

She still ignored us. The Child ran back to her and tried to drag her away but she wouldn't budge.

'She won't move,' the Child said helplessly.

I went over to Aladdin. 'Aladdin, this is all an illusion. The Wise Man told you that. We're in the Valley of the Mirage.'

Aladdin wasn't listening. Her ears pricked up. A black stallion appeared, scampering in and out of the trees. Aladdin whinnied happily and skittered after him.

'Aladdin!' we yelled, but she either didn't hear or didn't want to. She caught up to her new-found friend and they nuzzled each other then galloped off together, up and over a hill, and disappeared.

'Aladdin!' We ran after her for a little while but it was no use. She had gone. Tears streamed down the Child's cheeks.

'We've lost her.' His lips trembled. 'Oh, Aladdin . . . ' He sat down on the ground, utterly dejected.

'I'm sure she'll come back.'

'What if she doesn't? We can't stay here and wait for her. We'll be trapped.'

'Wait a minute,' I said. 'If this is all an illusion, then Aladdin is still with us. We've just fallen for the tricks. After all, it's the Valley of the Mirage and we're believing everything we see.'

'Of course,' said the Child, relieved.

'So, we'll just keep going and believe that Aladdin's really here.' The Child looked doubtful.

'Do you have any other suggestions?' I asked. He shook his head.

'What if she isn't really here?'

'Don't fear. Trust. And believe.'

That seemed to cheer him a little. We marched over to where we thought the path was.

'Let's go,' I said.

'Right. Come along, Aladdin.' My heart went out to him. He was trying to be so brave.

'Yes, come along, Aladdin,' I said forcefully.

And so we went further into the woods of the Valley of the Mirage . . .

The trees became thicker and wider as we walked until we found ourselves in a dark forest. The trees were so large and reached so high we could barely see the sky.

Finally, we had to stop. There were paths everywhere, leading further into the darkness. Strange birds cried evilly—black creatures like bats, but unlike any birds I'd ever seen.

'Don't fear. Trust. And believe,' the Child mumbled under his breath. I held his hand tightly.

'This is only a mirage. Take a deep breath and keep walking. Pretend it isn't there and it will go away.' I walked on and bumped straight into a tree.

'It is there!' The Child sounded very frightened. 'We're trapped!'

'No, we're not!' I replied angrily. 'You mustn't think that!' I sat him down under a tree. 'Now listen. We'll close our eyes and imagine this away. Like we did before.'

He stared at me, disbelieving.

'You're very brave all of a sudden.'

'I'm not being brave. I just want to get out of here.'

'Well, I'm frightened.'

'Come on, we've survived worse than this.' The Child didn't answer. He yawned.

'I'm so sleepy'. His eyes were blank. His head lolled on his shoulder.

'Don't go to sleep!' I shouted. I shook him, but it was as if he was drugged. His eyes closed and he fell back against the tree. I couldn't wake him.

'Please wake up. We've got to do this together.'

It was no use. And even as I tried to wake him I was aware that my own eyelids were getting heavy. An enormous tiredness overtook me.

'I must stay awake,' I murmured. But my limbs were so very stiff. I felt drugged. Then I, too, sank against the tree and fell asleep.

20

I HAD STRANGE DREAMS. WONDERFUL, MYSTERIOUS dreams. The figure of a beautiful woman advanced towards me. Her long white dress clung to her slim body. Her limbs were brown and her blonde hair tumbled wildly about her shoulders. She beckoned to me, smiling, and I walked towards her. I had no will of my own. She embraced me and kissed me gently on the cheek, then took my hand and led me away.

Over my shoulder, I saw the Child asleep by the tree but I no longer cared what happened to him. In the distance, I could see Aladdin again, galloping over the hills with her friend, the black stallion. But the thought of Aladdin didn't touch me. I had nothing to do with her.

I was completely powerless and I was enjoying it. There was something sensual about giving up my power and letting myself be led totally by someone else.

When the woman smiled at me, I forgot everything, lost in her beauty. Her mouth and eyes glistened—everything about her gleamed—there was a knowing air about her, and an availability, suggesting that anything I wanted she would do.

She led me to a river and slowly took me into the water. I held her, and we drifted below into the dark depths, yet I found I could breathe easily. The woman laughed and led me back to the surface.

I looked up and saw the Wise Man standing on the river bank.

'Wake up!' he yelled.

A force urged me to go towards the Wise Man but I wanted to stay with the woman.

'It's all illusion,' yelled the Wise Man. 'Wake up, before it's too late.'

As he said that, the woman took me under the water again and we drifted in the silent world. I could still hear the Wise Man's voice saying 'Wake up! Wake up!' and I began to struggle to get back to the surface. The woman held me back. Now I couldn't breathe. I was drowning. I fought desperately but the more I struggled the more the woman pushed me down, laughing all the while.

I saw stars. My lungs screamed with pain and I knew if I didn't get some air I would die. I hit at the woman savagely. She disappeared and I was alone, struggling in the water. I pushed my way up to reach the surface, gasping for breath. I swam desperately to the river bank and dragged myself onto it, my heart beating wildly.

The Wise Man was no longer there but I heard his voice in my ear.

'Wake up! Wake up!' I was so exhausted I wanted to sleep again. I clung to the Wise Man's voice and forced myself to sit up and open my eyes.

I was sitting under the tree with the Child and we were no longer in the forest. We were back on the path. I shook the Child awake.

'I was having the most wonderful dream,' he yawned, looking around. 'The forest has gone,' he said, amazed.

'It was an illusion. We have to be very careful in future.'

We looked up to see Aladdin standing across the path. The Child rushed to her and threw his arms around her.

'Aladdin! You didn't go away!'

I was shaken. How close we had come to being lost in the Valley of the Mirage.

'Thank you, Wise Man,' I muttered in silent prayer.

I took the Child's hand.

'Come on. Let's get out of here.'

21

'I DREAMT I WAS IN A GARDEN,' SAID THE CHILD sleepily as we walked along. 'It was a secret garden and I didn't want to leave. There were other children there and they were very friendly. It was a lovely dream.'

He was disappointed he had had to wake up. I understood how he felt. Now I knew the power of the Valley of the Mirage, I was very frightened. Next time we might not be so lucky.

'It was all part of the tricks they play here,' I said. 'Nothing is what it seems, so just remember that. It's all an illusion and we have to see past it to the real world. Otherwise we'll never get to the Silver City.'

'Is this the real world we're in now?' the Child asked anxiously.

'Yes!' Then I wondered if this, too, was an illusion. But the Wise Man had been there to help me. I trusted he would be there to guide us again if we were lost in the world of illusion.

'I'm hungry,' said the Child.

'Perhaps we can conjure up something?' He stared at me curiously. 'Well, this is the land of the mirage. That's

That's what they do here. The Wise Man told us,' I assured him.

'I'd like an ice-cream,' the Child announced excitedly.

We waited. Nothing happened.

'Maybe we have to be more specific,' I said.

'An ice-cream, with choc chips and honeycomb. A double, all dripping down the comb. So I can lick it off.' He closed his eyes in ecstasy. 'Hmmm! I can see it. I can really see it.' The ice-cream appeared in his hand.

'Wow!' he gasped. 'This is great!'

Aladdin tried to lick the ice-cream but the Child laughed and pulled it away.

'What can we get Aladdin to eat?' he asked.

'Aladdin's had enough to eat. She had all that grass.'

'Well, what do you want to eat?'

'A sandwich. No, a long French roll with ham, cheese and mustard. And a glass of fine white wine.'

'Yuk!' said the Child.

'Better for you than ice-cream,' I grinned.

'Doesn't taste as good, though.' He licked the ice-cream hungrily.

'Yes, that's what I'd like,' I said, dreaming of the French roll, which appeared in my hand a few seconds later, followed by a glass of really delicious wine.

'Hey, this is wonderful!' laughed the Child. 'No wonder people like to live here.' He finished his ice-cream greedily.

'Now a drink,' he demanded. He soon had his soft-drink. He was very excited and jumped around in little circles.

'A watch. I'd like a watch.' And he had a watch.

'A football,' he said. 'We'll play football.'

And he had his football. He kicked it around with gusto.

'Just a minute!' I took the football away. 'Listen to me!' We sat down together.

'This is why people get trapped in the Valley of the Mirage. Because they can have anything they want, and they forget why they came here. We musn't forget why we're here.'

'To get to the Silver City.'

'Yes! So don't ask for anything else. Let's just get out! It's too easy to be trapped.'

'All right . . . ' The Child was reluctant. 'Can I ask for one more thing?'

'No.'

He looked downcast and a little sulky.

'You can ask for anything you want, I can't stop you,' I said gently. 'But the more you get, the less you may want to leave.'

'Okay,' he nodded. 'I'm getting sucked into the mirage, aren't I?'

'Just a little,' I smiled.

So we set off again. We walked most of the day. Nothing disturbed us—no more illusions—and as night approached we began to feel a sense of relief.

'We must be out of the valley by now,' said the Child.

'I hope so.'

It had all been too easy, I thought. Why had we been allowed to leave so easily?

'Look, there's a barn,' said the Child. 'We can sleep there tonight.' He ran towards the barn, leading Aladdin behind him.

I stopped. Something was wrong. Something was very wrong indeed.

It was the same barn. We had travelled all day and come full circle—back to the same barn. We were trapped in the Valley of the Mirage.

22

NIGHT FELL. WE WERE VERY DEPRESSED. I SAT WITH MY arm around the Child.

'Couldn't we have some light?' he asked. 'We could conjure some up.'

'I don't want to use any of those tricks,' I said. 'Maybe that's why we ended up back in the barn—because we were tempted into trying for food.'

'Surely a light wouldn't hurt? It's very dark.' The poor little thing had been brave so many times, when I had been afraid. What harm was there in getting some light?

So we filled the barn with light and we felt a little less lonely. The Child was thoughtful. 'Why can't we get out of the valley just by thinking about it?'

'Perhaps we can,' I said, feeling excited.

If it was all an illusion—and we had the power to create it—why not create the illusion that we had escaped?

The Child was thoughtful again. 'It would still be an illusion. We'd still be in the valley.' He was right, of course.

'We're not really in the valley because if it's all a mirage it doesn't exist.'

'I wish I could believe that,' he said plaintively. 'It's getting to be pretty real.'

We sat thinking. We decided it couldn't do any harm to conjure up some food so we had some delicious pasta and more ice-cream for the Child. After a while we lay down to sleep.

'Goodnight, Aladdin!' we both chorused and closed our eyes.

'No!' I shouted.

'What is it?' The Child sat up quickly.

'We can't go to sleep. Remember what happened last time?'

He stared at me in horror.

'We've got to stay awake. If we fall asleep we may be lost,' I said firmly.

'I'm so tired.' The Child yawned again. 'We've walked all day.'

'Time doesn't exist here!' I said excitedly. 'It's all an illusion!'

'Yes?' he said, wondering what I was getting at.

'So, we'll imagine it's morning, that we've had a good sleep and we're rested and ready to leave.'

'Why not just imagine we've left?' he asked hopefully.

'We're going round in circles,' I sighed.

'It's all an illusion,' the Child said, yawning widely.

'Don't go to sleep!' I took his hand firmly. 'I imagine sunlight,' I announced. 'I imagine morning, and I imagine we feel rested and refreshed and ready to go . . . '

The Child didn't hear me. His eyes closed and he nodded off. Aladdin didn't move. She, too, was asleep.

'Don't sleep!' I shouted at them. I tried again to wake

the Child. He didn't stir. He was deep in sleep and still as death.

'Please wake up! Wake up, Aladdin!'

It was no use. Now I felt the familiar drugged feeling moving over my limbs, and my eyelids began to droop.

'No!' I yelled, and shook myself awake.

I tried to imagine sunlight, and rest, and a new day, but to do that I had to close my eyes and when I did that I wanted to sleep.

'Stay awake!'

I heard the voice of the Wise Man in my ear.

I took deep breaths and got up and moved around the barn. I went outside into the fresh air.

'Wake up, wake up,' I told myself, fighting the dreadful drowsiness that threatened to overcome me.

There in front of me was the woman in white, beckoning and smiling.

I turned away. Lights were moving through the trees. Crowds of people in medieval dress appeared, chanting and carrying lights through the streets. Streets?

I was now in a medieval town, and surrounded by crowds. It was so real, so vivid, and very beautiful. I wanted to stay there.

'No!' I yelled.

In a moment the town had gone and I was back outside the barn. The woman had gone, too. I felt stronger and not so tired.

I tried to breathe deeply, but even as I did, the terrible drugged feeling started to take over. I fought to keep my eyes open.

Some people emerged from the trees. They were all friends whom I hadn't seen for ages. They laughed and embraced me and took my arms to lead me away.

'No!' I yelled. 'No!'

And they were gone. My heart was beating fast but I knew I was stronger now. I turned back to the barn, not wishing to stay out in the night any longer, where there were too many tricks to be played on me.

The door of the barn blew shut as I approached. I tried to open it. It wouldn't budge. I banged loudly, calling to the Child, but to no avail.

There was laughter on the night air. Evil cackling surrounded me. Hands clawed at me, pulling my hair, scratching my face. I hit at them and backed away. The strange bat-like creatures flew at me from out of the forest.

I screamed, 'NO!' again, and suddenly all was silent. I tried to calm myself. I'd been able to stop some of the illusions. That gave me added strength.

'Well done,' said a voice, and a hand grasped my shoulder. I leapt in fright, only to find the Wise Man standing there.

'Wise Man,' I laughed. 'Am I glad to see you! I was so frightened. Aladdin and the Child have fallen asleep,' I told him. 'I can't wake them up.'

'Don't worry about them. Sleep will do them good,' said the Wise Man. 'Come with me.'

I hesitated. Surely I shouldn't leave them there? The Wise Man noticed my hesitation.

'Come, come,' he said. 'Do as I say.'

I started to go with him, and then I thought: the Wise Man wouldn't let me leave the Child and Aladdin asleep. He told me to stay awake.

'You're not the Wise Man,' I said. He looked surprised.

'Of course I am.'

'Prove it to me.'

The Wise Man looked hurt. 'If you insist. What do you want me to do?'

'Wake up the Child and Aladdin. Get them out of the barn.'

'But it's better if they sleep,' said the soothing voice of the Wise Man.

'No!' I shouted, testing him. And he disappeared.

I ran to the barn door and tried again to unlock it but it wouldn't open.

'Wake up, Child!' I called. 'Aladdin!'

I smelt smoke. Around the side of the barn flames were leaping across the wood. The whole wall was soon in flames.

Terrified, I screamed: 'NO! NO! NO!' The flames disappeared. I was now wide awake and strong. Stronger than before.

I breathed in the power surging through me.

'This is all an illusion!' I told myself. 'It cannot hurt me, it doesn't exist. I see past the illusion, I see past the Valley of the Mirage to the reality. I leave now with the Child and Aladdin!'

My body became full of light and I directed the light through the barn, and the barn began to dissolve. I filled the Child and Aladdin with light. They opened their eyes and looked at me.

The light within me grew and grew and flooded the landscape, and the trees and the houses and the people of the Valley of the Mirage disappeared, and suddenly we—the Child, Aladdin and I—were standing on a hill, and in front of us in the distance were the spires of the Silver City.

Behind us was the path we had been on before, and the Valley of the Mirage, although we couldn't see it. I knew we had come through it because all fear had left me and I was shimmering with light.

'We've done it!' yelled the Child, confirming our escape. 'We've come through the Valley of the Mirage!'

He threw his arms around my waist, and Aladdin did a few delighted little steps.

'Well done,' said the Wise Man.

He was sitting on a rock, combing his beard. For a moment, I hesitated.

'How do I know it's you?'

'Pshaw!' he said. And I knew it was he.

'It is you, isn't it?'

'I hope so,' he smiled, 'otherwise we're in serious trouble.' We all laughed. He winked at me.

'I think you've learnt enough to tell the unreal from the real.'

And I believed I had.

23

IT TOOK US MANY DAYS BUT SLOWLY WE CAME CLOSE to the Silver City. In that time I learnt much from the Wise Man.

This time he stayed with us for the entire journey and I remember it as a very happy time. We walked through innumerable valleys and villages and we met and talked with the people we found there. We were well looked after and food was always made available to us. All along our path people were expecting us, I don't know how. But in the company of the Wise Man I had ceased to be surprised at anything.

He never seemed to sleep. Sometimes, at night, I would find him sitting in a chair, his eyes wide open. He wouldn't see me staring at him. His spirit was elsewhere.

One night I sat by his side and waited for him to acknowledge me. After a while I couldn't keep awake any longer.

In the morning I was shaken awake by the Wise Man. I had fallen asleep with my head against his chair.

'Thank you for helping me,' he smiled.

'When?' I sleepily wondered what he was talking about.

'Last night.' He winked at me.

I followed him outside into the early morning sun.

'I don't understand, Wise Man. What do you mean?'

'Don't you remember anything after you fell asleep last night?' he asked. I couldn't remember very much. Only vague pictures flashed through my mind.

'Ah well. Perhaps that's for the best,' he said, in his most enigmatic manner.

'Please tell me what you mean,' I said.

'You see,' he was all patience. 'The soul has many adventures on many different levels. Not just in the body.'

'I know that. These adventures I have had with you haven't happened in the body, have they?'

'You're in a body now, aren't you?'

'Yes, but I'm not on the earth plane, am I?'

'So, last night we were on another plane. You helped me.'

'What did I do?'

'Oh well, if you don't remember, I won't tell you.'

'Please, Wise Man . . . '

'No, no. Sometimes it is best we don't remember. There's always a reason.'

No amount of coaxing from me would make him explain further.

'I do feel tired today,' I yawned. 'Did we do a lot of work last night?'

The Wise Man laughed.

'Only saved a few souls. It's good practice for you.'

Other days he was more forthcoming about his nightly trips. He went to other planets, he visited places where there were lost souls and helped them find the light. He helped souls who were dying on the earth plane and assisted them to the other side. He described to us where people went when they died and the different levels they could go to.

He kept us enthralled for days. Time flew and we didn't notice the long journey. Most of the time we were laughing too much to feel tired. When he was being funny the Wise Man was like a wicked child and made us laugh so much our sides ached. We felt joyously alive and happy.

Sometimes he'd allow Aladdin to fly us a little of the way. She hadn't flown at all since the day she'd rescued us and it appeared she would only fly if the Wise Man told her to, or if we were in trouble. Any time the Child or I asked her to fly just for fun, she resolutely refused to budge.

Oh what joy it was to fly again!

The Wise Man would watch us go and wave us off, telling us he would meet us ahead as he had work to do. We feared he wouldn't turn up but he was always there, waiting.

And so we flew through the blue skies on our beautiful white horse. Aladdin, her neck straining, her legs pounding the skies, would sometimes take us through the clouds and we could reach out and touch them.

Sometimes she wouldn't gallop, she would float, with just little kicks to keep her going. We would drift silently in space. Just the blue sky and the silence and the cool breezes wafting over us.

When we arrived, the Wise Man would be waiting and we would go to a house where he had friends. He had friends everywhere. We'd be looked after and fed, cleaned and made to feel very much at peace.

Soon I began to wake at night and I would feel impelled to join the Wise Man by his chair. I would sit watching him as he stared into the darkness, eyes wide open. I would feel his power and his love. My eyes would close and I would remember nothing else.

In the morning he winked conspiratorially. 'We did well last night, didn't we?'

I would be furious that I couldn't remember what had happened. He refused to tell me. But if he was happy with our work, I would be happy too.

On other mornings, when I had slept by his side, I would wake to find he was grim and in a mood. He didn't want to talk when he was in one of these moods, and if he looked at you, with those dark, brooding eyes of his, it was as if he had seen all the terrors of the world in you and you felt he was powerless to do anything. He knew the darkness you were capable of.

On those days I felt tired and I wondered if we had failed in our mission, whatever it was. However, he would soon cheer up and be his usual wise and funny self again.

They were wonderful days, travelling with the Wise Man. If I wondered about what lay ahead in the Silver City, I pushed the thought quickly aside. I was enjoying the good times and my travels, I'd worry about the future when it arrived.

Each day he would take me aside and talk to me. He seemed to have the wisdom of the world at his command. I knew he was preparing me for what lay ahead.

I was strong and happy, and looking back at the person

I had been at the beginning of our travels, I realised I'd changed enormously. But then the Wise Man's presence was so powerful, just being around him lifted your spirits.

One night when I joined him at his chair his eyes turned to me in the dark. They gleamed and looked into my heart.

'Are you ready for the next step?' he asked.

'What's that, Wise Man?' I gulped, and all my old fears surged through me.

'Tomorrow we reach the crossroads. There are four paths and one of them leads to the Silver City.' I knew what was coming. 'You must choose the right one.'

'How do I do that?' I said, my spirits sinking.

'You decide. No one else can make that decision for you.'

Fine, I thought, another decision!

'What if I fail?'

'There is no such thing as failure. Only results.'

'But what if I don't find the Silver City?' I asked.

'Then you will have taken another path. That's all right.'

'Where do the other paths lead?'

'I don't know. I've only been to the city.'

He smiled at me in the darkness, patting my face.

'Don't worry.'

Then he was silent. I knew he had gone on one of his journeys. I sat there, not feeling like sleep. Feeling only fear and darkness descending on my soul.

I was *very* worried.

24

The next morning we came over the crest of a hill and there was the Silver City. It was still in the distance, but closer than we'd ever seen it before. A wonderful place of glistening spires, reflecting the sun's rays.

It was the most impressive sight I had ever seen. Its tall, thin spires seemed to be made of glass. It was like a huge crystal—several huge crystals in a shining cluster. The city gave off a glow that filled the sky all around.

We stood silently in awe. The Wise Man mumbled something to himself and waved his hands in the air as though making an incantation.

The Child and Aladdin ran to the bottom of the hill. There were the four paths lying before us—the crossroads.

'Which way do we go?' the Child yelled over his shoulder. The Wise Man smiled benignly at me. I sighed, heavy with indecision.

'Goodbye,' he said.

'You're not coming with us?' Now I felt even worse.

'No, no,' he shook his head. 'Each of us must find our

own way to the Silver City, on our own path. I can't share your journey.'

'But I don't even know what to do when I get there,' I said with anguish.

'Worry about that *when* you get there.'

He shook my hand and we walked down the hill to Aladdin and the Child.

'The Wise Man isn't coming with us,' I said dejectedly.

'What? *Again*!' The Child sighed heavily.

The Wise Man laughed, 'I have other things to do. You'll be all right on your own.'

'I know,' said the Child. 'Don't fear. Trust. And believe.'

'See?' the Wise Man said to me, 'it's really very easy.'

I didn't laugh. What if I took the wrong path?

'You can still turn back, you know.' The Wise Man had read my mind. 'No one's forcing you to do this.'

'Can anything happen to us?' The Child looked worried.

'Only if you believe it can.'

I looked behind, to the way we'd come. Should I go back? I knew I couldn't. For better or for worse, I had agreed to come this far and I knew I must keep going.

'We'll be all right,' I told the Child bravely, but with more conviction than I felt. 'Nothing bad will happen to us.'

I turned to the Wise Man with sinking heart.

'When will we see you again?'

'Oh, that depends.'

'On what?'

'On which path you take. Remember the path to God

is straight and narrow. Many are called but few are chosen.'

Great, I thought. Now he's throwing biblical quotations at me.

'We'll see you again, Wise Man, I know that,' the Child told him. The Wise Man patted his cheek and the Child threw his arms around the Wise Man's legs, holding tight, not wanting to let go.

'Be brave,' said the Wise Man. 'A brave man can overcome. Only fear stops you.'

'We're not afraid,' the Child answered bravely. 'Are we, Aladdin?'

The horse neighed and nuzzled the Wise Man, putting her head down to be patted. The Wise Man whispered something in Aladdin's ear. She waved her tail and did a few little backward steps.

'So,' said the Wise Man. 'Goodbye for now.'

I felt great sadness. I feared I would never see him again.

'Goodbye. Thank you.' Words could never express my thanks for what he had given me—even though I was angry that he was leaving just when we needed him most.

The Wise Man walked back up the hill, smiled, waved, and disappeared. The Child and I stared sadly at each other.

Once again we were on our own.

25

We sat on the ground in front of the crossroads and waited. By midday the sun was very hot. There was no shade anywhere. I sat staring hopelessly at the four paths, not knowing which one to take.

The old, familiar heaviness that I always felt when I had to make a decision settled on me. The fear of making a mistake. I was full of self-pity and starting to be convinced I would make the wrong decision anyway.

This was too much to ask of anyone. How could I be expected to work out which path to take? They all looked exactly the same. They all looked as though they led to the Silver City. But of course they didn't.

Aladdin and the Child watched in silence, aware of my inner turmoil.

Finally the Child said: 'I'm getting very hot. Are we going to sit here all day?'

I got up wearily. 'I might as well toss a coin.'

'If we go the wrong way we can always come back,' said the Child cheerfully.

He'd given me an idea. 'There are four paths, and three

of us. Why don't we each take a path and follow it for an hour? By then we should know if we're on the wrong path and we'll come back and meet here and exchange notes.'

The Child looked at me.

'You mean, go by myself?' He was very reluctant.

'Only a little way.'

He ignored my suggestion. 'Why not get Aladdin to fly over the paths; then she'll be able to tell us which is the right one.'

What a good idea. 'Will you do that for us, Aladdin?' I asked. We got on her back. She didn't move. No amount of persuasion would get her to fly. She obviously had her instructions from the Wise Man and she wasn't going to make things easy for us.

We got off. 'Thanks a lot, Aladdin,' I said crankily. Aladdin blinked at me as though to say: it's your decision, you work it out.

'So, it's back to my original suggestion.'

'Go on our own?' asked the Child, with trepidation.

'Just to check it out. How else are we going to decide?'

'Toss a coin, like you suggested.'

'We'll toss a coin to see which path we *each* take,' I said. 'Aladdin can choose one of the two in between.'

The Child looked grim. He didn't like the idea at all.

I tossed the coin. Heads. I would go right and the Child would take the left path. The Child and Aladdin didn't move.

'Off you go,' I waved at them. 'We'll meet back here in two hours.'

'I want to go with you.' The Child's lips trembled.

'You'll be all right.'

'How do you know? Anything could happen to me and there'll be nobody to help me.'

'Just go a little way and come back and report. Like a soldier.'

'I'm not a soldier.'

'Yes, you are. A brave soldier. Like Aladdin. Which path do you want to take, Aladdin?' I pointed to the two paths between the ones we were taking. Aladdin turned away disdainfully.

'She doesn't want to go alone either,' said the Child. I tried to push Aladdin forward, giving her a slap on her rump. 'Go on, Aladdin. Please.'

She wouldn't move.

'Look,' I said angrily, 'if you don't do this for me, we'll never find the way.'

'Let's imagine we've found the way,' said the Child, 'like we did before.' He would obviously think of any ruse to avoid going off on his own.

So we sat down, closed our eyes and tried to imagine. But I couldn't relax. I was too worried. The Child opened one eye.

'It won't work if you think bad thoughts.'

'I'm not thinking bad thoughts.'

'You're not full of light. Your body is very dark.' I looked down and could see the cloud of worry around me.

We closed our eyes again and I imagined us standing at the crossroads, feeling confident, knowing which way to choose. I tried to bring in the light but I was too full of fear.

'I can't do it.'

But the Child was radiating light and so was Aladdin.

She did a few little joyous steps in the air.

'It's there!' The Child pointed to the last path on the left. 'That's the path to the Silver City.'

'How do you know?'

'I just know!' He tried to drag me towards the path.

'Now listen!' I said, and stopped him. 'Let's explore the other three paths first. Just to be sure.'

'No, no,' he shouted. 'It's to the left. I know it is. Trust me.'

'Only if you trust me first.'

'Oh, why won't you believe me. It's that one.'

'All right. Wait here. I'll try the one on the right first and explore it a little bit.'

'No, no. It's the one on the left, I tell you!' The Child was getting red in the face.

'Calm down. Just wait here.'

So I took the path to the right. I had made my decision.

26

It was an ordinary path. It looked like any other path. I couldn't see very far ahead, the path kept turning sharply to the right. Soon there was bush everywhere and the path became dense and tangled.

I remembered the words of the Wise Man: 'The path to God is straight and narrow,' and I thought: this can't be it. All my instincts told me it wasn't. Perhaps the Child was right.

My ego felt a little bruised. It was disconcerting to think that the Child seemed to have been able to pick the path to the Silver City so easily. Why couldn't I have done that? I was too full of fear, I answered myself. But then, I thought, we don't know that the Child is correct. It couldn't be so easy, surely?

I turned back, trusting my instincts that I wasn't on the right path. I ran to the crossroads.

The Child and Aladdin were gone. I cursed. I'd told them to wait for me.

'Child? Aladdin?' I yelled. There was no answer. It was silent on that hot and dusty road. Perhaps they'd gone on the path to the left. The Child had been so convinced it was the path to the Silver City. I was about to follow when I heard the Child screaming in the distance.

His voice was coming from the path next to the one I had just travelled. I ran along this path, hearing the Child's desperate screams get closer.

I turned a corner and ran into a huge spider's web. I screamed in fright. I hit at it wildly, desperately trying to brush the strands off my hair and my clothes. I pushed and struggled through it to escape but the more I struggled the more entangled I became.

It was the most terrifying experience of my life. I have always been afraid of spiders. Now I was caught in a giant spider's web and I could hardly move. The more I struggled the more the web stuck to me. I could feel sweat on my brow. I tried to calm myself. Panic wasn't getting me anywhere. I took deep breaths. I forced myself to open my eyes.

There were webs everywhere. Ahead of me was the Child, also caught in the webs. He saw me and cried pathetically, 'Help me!'

'Calm down. Can you move at all?'

'Of course I can't move, otherwise I wouldn't be screaming.'

'All right, all right. Stay calm. I'll think of something. I told you to stay where you were,' I added angrily.

'I was only trying to help you. You wanted to explore the other paths and you told me to be brave, so I was.'

'That was very brave,' I said.

'Yes. And look what happened.'

'No need to rub it in. At least we know this isn't the right path,' I said.

'I want to get out of here.' His voice trembled. 'It's all sticky and wet.'

'I'll get you out. Don't worry.'

I tried to push towards the Child but the webs held me tightly. They clung to every part of my body. Any attempt to move made them stick more firmly.

I was terribly afraid. I musn't panic, I thought. I must stay calm. I took some more deep breaths.

'If you'd only listened to me! I told you which path to take!' cried the Child.

'We don't know if it was the path to the Silver City. It might have been worse than this.'

That shut him up.

I looked around. The web had been spun in huge circles that blocked the path. The circles grew and grew up to the treetops, and then over my head in continuing circles to where the Child was, and beyond the Child they formed into a huge circular tunnel.

My heart went cold. What had spun these webs? Was it in the tunnel behind the Child? Again I tried to move. This time very slowly. I attempted to climb on to one of the rungs of the circle to push my way out. I found the rung was very strong and could hold my weight.

Slowly I disentangled myself from some of the webs that were stuck to me. I managed to drag myself up to the next rung. I stood on it and held on to the line of web above me to keep my balance.

'Watch what I'm doing!' I called to the Child. He watched me intently then tried to do the same thing.

'I can't do it. I can't move,' he sobbed.

I knew I would have to go in and help him. I was terrified. I didn't want to go any further into those webs.

'Help me!' His little face was piteous.

I forgot my fear and began to climb along the rungs towards him.

Then there was a strange rumbling noise. The webs began to shake.

'What's that?' the Child cried in terror.

Two huge eyes were peering at me from inside the webbed tunnel. The webs began to shake violently. A venomous, stinking wind blew me backwards and I fell off the rungs and became caught again in sticky webs near the ground.

The Child screamed. He'd seen what I'd seen.

The biggest spider in the world was emerging from the tunnel. A huge, black giant that made us look like ants. Its enormous legs were slowly, inexorably creeping towards the Child.

'NO-O-ooo!' I screamed. I wanted to help the Child and I couldn't do anything. I was paralysed with fear.

'Help me! Help me!' The Child struggled wildly, his face a mask of terror. In a second, the huge black legs had picked him up like a piece of meat and dragged him back into the tunnel.

After a while his screams stopped. The awful wind ceased. I began to cry. My whole body shook. I wanted to throw up.

'God, help me,' I moaned. 'Please save him.' But I didn't believe anything could save the Child now.

I struggled wildly through the webs. Somehow my fear and panic gave me enormous strength. I finally managed to climb through the rungs to the path. Then I ran for my life to the crossroads.

I sat in the dust, under the hot sun, and my sweat mingled with my tears. I shook, and sobbed hysterically.

There was a soft nuzzle at my shoulder. Aladdin's eyes were dark and sad, as they looked into mine.

'Oh, Aladdin, where were you?'

In answer to my question she scampered towards the first path I had entered.

'Did you try to follow me?'

She nodded and waved her tail.

'And you heard the screams?'

She whinnied.

'Aladdin, I think we've lost him.'

Aladdin nuzzled me, pushing at me with her face. I thrust her away. I wanted to wallow in my misery.

'Let me cry, Aladdin. I can't help it.'

Aladdin whinnied louder. She pawed the ground. She wouldn't let me sit crying in the road. She forced me to stand up.

'What do you want?' She waved her head and stamped her little feet again.

'Can we save him, Aladdin? Can you save him?'

She whinnied, as if in agreement.

'No, we can't risk your life, Aladdin.' I sat down again. She nuzzled me more insistently.

'What do you want me to *do*?' I cried. 'You want to try to save him?' She nodded her head, stamping her hooves.

I got on her back. 'Fly, Aladdin!' I said.

She didn't move. I stroked her, I pushed her, even kicked her gently. She wouldn't budge. What did she want from me? I began to sob again in helpless frustration. Aladdin whinnied irritably.

'What? What is it? If you don't want to fly, what do you want to do?'

Aladdin glared at me balefully.

I thought hard. Suddenly I could see the Wise Man in my head. He was smiling at me and saying, 'Wake up!' What a fool I was.

We had saved him from the moving cliffs. I remembered how he had saved me in the Valley of the Mirage. Now it was my turn to save the Child. That was what Aladdin was trying to tell me.

I closed my eyes and breathed deeply. I filled myself with the light. I saw the spider's webs in front of me and, with the light streaming from me, I pushed them aside. I moved through them to the tunnel.

I filled the tunnel with light and it began to dissolve. I saw the Child lying beside the huge spider. He stirred and moaned softly. He was alive.

I opened my eyes.

'He's still alive, Aladdin!' and I saw we were in the air. Aladdin was floating not far above the ground. My body was full of light, as was Aladdin's. I knew we could do anything. We were all-powerful.

'Go for it, Aladdin!' I shouted.

Then we were flying over the path and towards the tunnel. All I could see and feel was golden light. I sent it into the tunnel and over the spider, who looked up at me with its evil eyes. With all the light I could muster I looked into those eyes, and slowly the spider began to back away, further into its lair, until it disappeared.

Aladdin hovered over the Child.

'Child,' I called. 'Wake up!' The Child stirred. I filled him with light. He leapt up.

'Quickly,' I said. Reaching down to him I pulled him onto Aladdin's back and we rose into the sky and flew away.

27

We were back at the crossroads.

'Are you all right?' I brushed the Child down and picked off sticky bits of web. He smiled weakly. He was very groggy. I laid him gently on the ground.

'Put your hands around my head,' he directed. I did so, puzzled. 'Now heal me.'

'Did the spider bite you?' I asked, horrified.

'I don't think so. I just feel very, very tired.' He slurred his words as though he were drugged. His little face was very pale. I couldn't lose him now when we had survived so much.

'Fill me with light,' he mumbled as his eyes closed. I held his head in my hands. I tried to draw light into my body and give it to him.

I pictured the cells getting better and his body glowing with health. I saw the spider unable to harm him, saw him totally protected from any poison and I trusted that he was well.

The Child opened his eyes.

'That's better!' He stretched his arms. I was surprised he'd recovered so quickly. 'You're getting good at this.'

He sounded just like the Wise Man.

I embraced him, so grateful to have him alive. Aladdin nudged her little face between ours.

'It's Aladdin we have to thank.' We hugged Aladdin. 'She gave me the courage to save you.'

'But you would have done it, anyway,' the Child said, taking my hand. I smiled.

'Aladdin reminded me of what I could do.'

I still didn't know which of the two remaining paths to take. The Child read my mind.

'Let's go to the Silver City.' He didn't have any doubts. He dragged me towards the path on the left.

'We don't know that's the path to the Silver City.'

'I do! Why won't you believe me?' I wished I had his childlike trust but I was still doubtful.

'Shouldn't we explore the other path first? We have to be sure.'

'The Wise Man said the path would choose us, and it has. We meditated and got the message.'

'*You* meditated,' I said. 'And I didn't get the message.'

As we talked, Aladdin moved curiously towards the second of the two remaining paths and wandered out of sight.

'There you are,' I said. 'Maybe Aladdin knows which path to take!' I started to follow.

'No, don't go in there!' he warned, and tried to stop me.

'Why?'

'I just have a feeling we shouldn't.' He looked worried.

'You stay here, then, and rest. You've been through enough today.' He was obviously still distressed. And who wouldn't be, after what he'd been through?

'No! I'm coming with you!' He held on to me, determined not to be left alone. So we walked onto the path.

We followed it around several narrow little bends then, unexpectedly, it opened up. It stretched endlessly, as far as the eye could see. Aladdin was nowhere in sight.

'Oh, Aladdin,' moaned the Child. 'Where is she?'

'She'll come back. She wouldn't leave us,' I comforted him. But I wasn't so sure.

'Anything could happen to her! We don't know what's out there.'

'The Silver City certainly isn't,' I sighed. 'We'd be able to see it.'

'I told you it was on the other path!'

I smiled ruefully. 'I'm sorry I didn't listen to you.'

There were no glistening spires on the horizon. Just a weird, empty landscape. And where was Aladdin? Surely she wouldn't leave us? But, I reminded myself, she had before, in the Valley of the Mirage. Who knew what illusions lay on this strange, seemingly deserted path?

'Perhaps she's flying?' The Child scanned the sky hopefully. 'From up there she could easily see which path leads to the Silver City.'

I didn't think so. She would have taken us with her.

'She only seems to fly when we're in trouble,' I replied. We continued walking, and as we walked it got hotter. And hotter. The air was heavy and I had trouble breathing. The Child, too, was gasping.

'There's something wrong here. You were right,' I said, stopping to catch my breath. 'Let's not go any further.' As I spoke, the Child ran forward and disappeared.

I couldn't believe it. He had vanished before my eyes.

'Where are you?' There was no answer.

I slowly stepped forward to the spot where he'd vanished. My foot disappeared. I stepped back quickly. My foot reappeared. I tried again. The same thing happened.

There was an invisible wall across the path and when you crossed it you entered into another world.

If I followed the Child, would we be able to get back? I tentatively pushed part of my body through the invisible screen and watched it disappear. For a moment I was half in one world and half in the other.

I could see the path in front of me stretching ahead endlessly, and yet I could put my hand through the invisible barrier to another place behind.

I felt around with my hand, on the other side.

'Child, are you there?'

Another hand grabbed mine. A soft, clammy hand. I screamed, quickly pulled my hand away, and stepped back onto the path. I was shaking. Who, or what, was on the other side?

'Child? Are you there?' There was no reply. 'Aladdin? Where are you?' Now I was very worried. I stood helplessly outside the invisible wall, not knowing what to do.

I had to go in and find them. Once again, I cursed myself for opting to travel with the Wise Man and I cursed him for what he'd got me into. He was never there when you needed him!

I didn't want to meet whoever was hiding behind the wall. I crept to the other side of the path. After a moment's hesitation I cautiously put my hand through the wall again. Terrified, I started to pull it back but no one grabbed it. I waited. Nothing.

I was about to step through when something made me

turn around. The Wise Man was there, shaking his head, warning me not to go.

'Wise Man!' I ran to him joyfully but the picture faded. I touched empty space.

Was this a trick, or was the Wise Man trying to warn me, reaching out, from wherever he was, to help me? If so, I thought grudgingly, why didn't he stay and really help?

I moved back to the invisible wall. Again I felt the Wise Man's presence behind me. This time I couldn't see him but I was certain he was warning me not to go into the other world.

'I have to help them,' I appealed to him desperately.

The Wise Man's voice in my ear whispered: 'You must go on alone.'

'No! I can't leave them!' I shouted.

Again I heard the Wise Man's voice. 'Only the chosen can enter the Silver City.'

I felt his presence so strongly, but I couldn't see him. Then I thought: perhaps, after all, this was only another trick and it wasn't the Wise Man talking to me.

I stepped up to the invisible wall and put my hand through. Another hand took hold of it, this time in a vice-like grip. I yelled and tried to pull away but whoever—whatever—was holding me was determined not to let go. I struggled furiously. I thought my hand was going to be wrenched off at the wrist.

I was stronger, however. I pulled and pulled, and with an enormous yank managed to get free. The effort sent me reeling backwards. I fell onto the hot, dusty road. I lay there, breathing heavily and feeling dejected and miserable.

The Wise Man's words echoed in my ear.

'You must go on alone.'

I couldn't go on alone. I couldn't leave the Child and Aladdin. I couldn't. Yet I might never reach the Silver City if I got lost in the mysterious world on the other side of the invisible wall.

The thought of leaving my friends made my heart break. Tears rolled down my cheeks. I sat in the dirt and sobbed.

I don't know how long I sat there. I cried until I had no tears left, then I struggled wearily to my feet and brushed myself down.

I would go on alone. I had to. There was no choice. With a heavy sigh, I turned away from the invisible wall and silently trudged along the path towards the crossroads.

I looked back only once. I shouted to the empty air: 'Child? Aladdin? I'll come for you one day. I promise.'

There was, of course, no answer. I returned to the crossroads, feeling lonelier than I had ever been in my life.

I looked at the path on the left. The path the Child had chosen. I felt I didn't have the heart to go on, yet a force stronger than me was pushing me forward. If I got to the Silver City and did whatever I had to do, then I would find a way to rescue the Child and Aladdin.

Taking a deep, miserable breath, feeling tremendously guilty at leaving my friends to whatever fate awaited them, I turned onto the left-hand path. The path to the Silver City.

It seemed straightforward enough. A dirt track like the others. I moved slowly and with trepidation, afraid of what I might find this time. The path took sharp bends.

Like the other paths, you had no idea what was around the corner until you fell upon it.

As I walked I could hear the sound of the sea. My spirits lifted slightly. If there was a beach, I would swim. I was hot, dusty and exhausted. It had been a terrifying day, to say the least.

The sound of the sea was closer. Excited, I began to run towards it. I could smell the salt air.

'I'm on my way!' I yelled triumphantly. 'To the Silver City!'

I ran faster, turned a corner, and almost fell off a cliff.

The path came to an abrupt halt. It finished at the edge of a clifftop. Far, far below was the pounding sea. Water stretched ahead of me into infinity.

I was devastated. This was not the path to the Silver City. If it was, I'd have to swim to it, and that was impossible. The city couldn't be seen on the skyline, even in the far distance.

I sat down at the edge of the cliff. I was extremely depressed. I had explored all four paths and none led to the Silver City. I'd been tricked.

'Help me, Wise Man,' I cried out to the sky.

No answer came. I was on my own. Really on my own this time.

For the moment I was too exhausted and beaten to care. I lay down, and to the sound of the waves crashing on the rocks, I closed my eyes and slept.

28

I DIDN'T SLEEP WELL. I HAD STRANGE DREAMS.

In the first dream, the Child and Aladdin appeared to me. The Child laughed delightedly as he rode Aladdin across a landscape of soft green fields and rolling hills. I was miffed to see they were getting along very well without me. I called out. They turned and the Child waved. They galloped towards me but as they came close I found I couldn't touch them.

I put my hand out to them. There was an invisible barrier through which I couldn't pass.

'We're all right,' the Child told me. 'Don't worry. You have to go on alone.'

'I can't!' In the dream I was sobbing. 'I can't do any more. I've failed. There's no way to get to the Silver City.'

'You can do it.' The Child smiled bravely at me. Aladdin whinnied and did a few steps in the air.

'I want to be with you,' I cried.

'We'll always be together,' said the Child. 'But you have to go on.'

'You were wrong about the path. It doesn't lead to the Silver City.'

'I wasn't wrong,' the Child answered. 'It was the right path for me.'

'But I can't take it, you mean? Then where is the right path for me?' I asked desperately.

The Child only smiled and waved.

'Don't fear. Trust. And believe.' And he and Aladdin rode away.

I woke up crying: 'Come back. Please come back.'

It was almost nightfall. I was alone on a clifftop, high above the sea, miles from anywhere.

'Which is the right path for me?' I whispered hopelessly to the sea below.

I didn't care any more. I was hungry and exhausted. I could hear the Child's voice: 'Don't fear. Trust. And believe.' But something in me had given up. I went back to sleep.

I dreamt of the giant spider. I was trapped again in the spider's sticky webs, and it was crawling towards me. I hit at it wildly and tried to escape but I couldn't move. The spider loomed over me, its eyes glittering wickedly, and it opened its huge mouth to swallow me.

'No!' I screamed and woke up, shivering. It was night and it was pitch black. I could hear the sea below but I couldn't see anything in front of me. I was frightened. I thought I should move away from the cliff and find somewhere safe to sleep.

I decided to make my way back to the crossroads.

As I moved from the edge of the cliff I heard a hissing noise and something slithered across the path in front of me. A large snake rose up, hissing, its little narrow eyes glistening in the dark.

I backed away quickly, feeling nervously along the edge

of the cliff, terrified I was going to fall off. There was nowhere to hide on the cliff, and nothing but the sea below.

'This is great!' I thought. 'Now I'm trapped on a cliff, with a snake!'

The hissing had stopped. I didn't know where the snake was. I stood near the edge of the cliff and tried to be very still but my whole body was trembling.

I heard the Child's voice again: 'Don't fear.'

I was afraid. Very afraid. Too frightened to sleep, too tired to stay awake.

I thought again about the four paths to the Silver City. The Wise Man had talked about the straight and narrow path and told me it would choose me. Nothing had chosen me, except perhaps the snake—wherever it was, lurking in the dark, waiting to pounce. Which was the way to the Silver City? There had to be an answer.

I was too weary to stand hovering on the cliff edge any longer so I sat down.

'If you're going to bite me, do it! I don't care,' I yelled to the snake. 'I've had enough.'

In answer, there was a slithering sound near me. For a moment I felt fear. There was sweat on my brow, my armpits were wet, but I didn't move. I said: 'Oh for heaven's sake, go away. Leave me alone.'

I really didn't care any more. Let what was going to happen, happen. I sat waiting to be pounced on. But nothing happened.

I took deep breaths of fresh salt air, felt the light sea-breeze on my face and my spirits lifted a little.

'Trust,' came the Child's voice in my ear.

'All right,' I answered. 'I trust. If I'm meant to get to

the Silver City, I'll get there. But I'm not going to do any more. It will have to come to me.'

And as I said that I knew the answer. Of course! None of the paths led to the Silver City. The path was inside. Inside me. I had stopped the cliffs moving with the power of my thought. I had made Aladdin fly. Could I take myself to the Silver City by imagining it?

A doubting little voice said: 'You weren't able to get your friends out of the Invisible World.'

'I'm sure I could have,' I answered back, shouting to the dark sky. 'But I have to go on alone. That's part of the plan.'

And I knew I could go on.

'I *will* go on! I will go to the Silver City!'

Strength surged through me. Anything was possible.

And I heard the Child's voice: 'Believe.'

'I believe!' I yelled.

I breathed in and filled my body with light and I didn't fear any more. I trusted and I believed that I already knew the way to the Silver City.

The light filled the air around me and pushed away the night. I saw the snake coiled up next to my feet, sound asleep, and I wasn't at all afraid.

'I'm in the Silver City *now*!' I said.

In my mind, the silver crystals glistened and grew brighter and brighter and I moved closer and closer until the brightness was overwhelming, and I smiled radiantly.

I opened my eyes. I was standing before the Silver City.

29

AND SO I CAME TO THE SILVER CITY.

When I opened my eyes I saw glass everywhere. There were two suns in the sky, their beams reflecting in the towering glass buildings. All was light. The Silver City glittered with it.

I was standing outside the city gates. High, imposing glass doors in a golden frame. Behind the gates the spires of the glass buildings soared above me. I stared in amazement at the two suns in the crystal blue sky. I could feel the energy coming from them.

The Silver City was alive with energy. It filled my body, my mind and my heart until I was radiant with it. This time the light did not fade. For as long as I remained in the Silver City, I would reflect its glow.

The city was built on a mountain, and the green land fell away from it down to the sea. The vegetation was lush, amid fields of wondrously coloured flowers.

It was a place of enchantment. I knew already that I would never want to leave. I breathed a sigh of contentment and was happier than I'd ever been.

'Thank you for bringing me here,' I said aloud, thanking

both God and the Wise Man. I was grateful I had finally reached the Silver City and felt honoured to be there. My only sadness was that the Child and Aladdin weren't with me to see for themselves this most beautiful of places.

As I stood before the city—my feelings a mixture of awe and gratitude—the imposing gates opened and a girl emerged. She was tiny, with long dark hair and, I guessed, only about 17 or so. She wore white robes. Her skin shone with health and she glowed with goodness and purity.

In her hands she held a small globe, set in gold, which she carried gently towards me. A golden flame burned brightly within the globe.

The girl smiled a lovely smile.

'Thank you for coming to us. We are so glad to see you,' she said.

'I am very glad to be here,' I replied.

She smiled again and led me to the glass gates. As we were about to enter, she turned and handed me the golden globe.

'This is yours. To light your way. Be careful with it. Do not let the flame go out.'

I groaned inwardly. Was this yet another test? I didn't think I could take any more. At the same time I heard a voice in my ear. The voice of the Wise Man said: 'Nothing is ever given to you that you do not have the strength to bear.'

So I took the globe, steadied myself, and entered the Silver City.

A guard at the gate smiled as though he knew me. The streets were crowded with people. Everybody glimmered with light, their bodies almost transparent.

As we moved through the crowd they smiled and waved to me as if we were old friends. I couldn't see into the towering glass buildings on either side of the street but now that I was closer to them I could feel them pulsating with energy.

'My name is Leela,' the girl told me as we walked along. 'I am to be your guide in the Silver City.'

'Thank you,' I said. 'Where are we going?'

'To the palace of the Wise Ones. They wish to meet you.'

My heart leapt. 'Will the Wise Man be there?'

Leela looked puzzled. 'They are all Wise Men,' she replied.

'But there is one particular Wise Man who sent me here.'

'I don't know,' she smiled. 'We will see.'

We moved up the cobbled street. The cobbles were also made of glass. High on a hill stood a white palace.

'That is the palace of the Wise Ones,' said Leela. As we walked up the hill the air became clearer and lighter. I had difficulty breathing. Leela laughed. 'You will get used to it. Here the air is finer because we are entering another dimension.' I nodded, gasping and taking deep breaths. Leela laughed again. 'You must certainly be able to breathe up here, otherwise you wouldn't be able to visit the Wise Men.'

Impressed by the honour being accorded me, I immediately felt easier and found if I relaxed and breathed gently I could manage the walk up the hill.

The flame flickered in the globe I was carrying, shaken by my attempts at breathing.

'Careful,' said Leela. 'Remember the light.' I had

forgotten. I walked very carefully, breathing away from the flame. How long was I going to have to carry this thing around, I wondered?

'The Wise Men will tell you,' said Leela.

'What?' I said, startled that she had read my mind.

'Here, all thoughts are visible,' she continued. 'We are beings of the light. We are all one, we share the light and so we share thoughts. And a dark thought is easy to read because a little bit of light disappears from you.'

I was embarrassed she had caught me out.

'But you would not be here if you hadn't got rid of most of your dark thoughts.' She smiled, amused at my discomfort.

I allowed myself a little pat on the back. Yes, I thought proudly, I had got rid of a lot of dark thoughts along the way. Well, some. I'd had to, to survive. The positive thoughts, the light, that had rescued me every time.

I smiled back at Leela. 'I'll try not to have any more dark thoughts.'

'Don't try,' she said. 'You don't have to *try*. Just rest in the light. It's very easy.'

She made it sound easy. A voice within me, a nagging little put-upon voice, said: It hasn't been too easy for me.

I shrugged it off. Up here in the heights of the Silver City, negativity had no place. I couldn't be bothered to give it any energy.

Leela laughed, a delightful gurgling little laugh. She had again read my mind.

'You're very funny.'

'Yes, I am,' I replied ruefully, but I laughed with her.

The palace of the Wise Men was simply a large white building with white doors and large windows surrounded by glorious gardens. The place shone with a powerful light and was alive with energy.

The main doors slid open as we approached and we entered a large hall with seats on either side. At the end of the aisle, on a raised dais, was a long table, and there sat ten men, all in white robes, all reflecting light, so it seemed as if the whole room was enclosed in a golden ball of light. I looked hopefully for the Wise Man but he wasn't among the ten.

Leela knelt before the dais. The man in the centre of the group stood up and stepped forward to meet Leela. He patted her head gently. She rose and stepped aside.

Now the man looked at me with eyes unlike any I'd ever seen. They were like blue diamonds. He lifted a finger and beckoned to me.

'Come forward,' he said.

30

I MOVED FORWARD TO THE DAIS. THE WISE MEN ALL smiled at me benignly, their faces kind and compassionate. I felt love in their presence—a love that was unconditional and did not judge me.

I looked again into the eyes of the Wise Man who had beckoned to me. He was tall and imposing, with greying hair. He appeared to be almost transparent, a being of light. The light streamed from his extraordinary eyes and when he beckoned to me I was impelled to kneel before him, as Leela had.

'You have done well,' said the man. 'Very few find the Silver City.'

I thanked him and stayed silent. I sensed that anything I had to say would be irrelevant. Anyway, I was sure the Wise Men could all see into my soul and knew me better than I knew myself. I noticed the flame within the globe had grown brighter. I held the globe carefully to my chest.

'Rest a while with us,' said the man, 'before you return to the Valley of the Lost Souls.'

My heart sank. 'Must I do that?' I asked.

'Isn't that what you set out to do?' He smiled at me kindly.

I had struggled so long and so hard to reach the Silver City I had begun to think that when I reached it my quest would be over. That my finding of the Silver City *was* the quest and would somehow save the lost souls!

'I wasn't sure,' I said lamely. 'I only knew I had to find the Silver City.'

'To bring back the gold, my son.'

'What is the gold?'

'You will find out in time.' The Wise Man smiled again and tapped me on the head. I got up, holding the flame in the globe carefully.

'Now is the time to rest from your labours and gain new strength for the end of your journey. We will talk again.'

'Thank you,' I said.

'No, no. It is we who must thank you,' he smiled.

'I haven't done anything,' I said modestly.

'You have trusted and believed. You have found that is the way to the Silver City. It is also the way to complete your journey and return home.'

'Thank you,' I mumbled again, overcome with love for this man. As I moved away from the dais, all the other Wise Men beamed and applauded. I felt my cheeks flush. Leela, grinning at me proudly, led me out of the Great Hall.

Leela took me to her house. It was a small glass dome by the sea and was surrounded by a garden, with all sorts of colourful flowers, and a path leading to the beach, directly in front of it.

Inside, the house was simple and uncluttered. A few

rugs were scattered about, a table, a few chairs, a long white couch, and all the walls were made of glass. There were no windows, but Leela pressed a button and the glass walls slid aside, as did the ceiling, so we were almost living in the open air when we wanted to.

Delightful perfumes wafted through the house. Breathing them in made you happy and filled your heart with contentment.

But then, from the moment I entered the Silver City, I knew only joy.

I looked out at the sun sparkling on the blue sea—bluer than any other sea. All the colours in the Silver City were richer and more abundant than any I had ever seen. I breathed in the sea air and gave thanks. I was almost completely happy. If only the Child and Aladdin could have been with me.

'They are quite safe,' said Leela, once again reading my thoughts. 'They are content and will wait for your return.'

Suddenly, on the wall, as though on a screen, I could see Aladdin and the Child. But this was more than a film. It was three-dimensional. They were riding towards me and I stepped forward to meet them. To my surprise, I was in the scene with them and I could touch them.

The Child and I embraced and I hugged Aladdin. Tears rolled down my face.

'Are you all right?' I asked.

'Of course we are,' said the Child sturdily. 'We're having a wonderful time.'

'Who's looking after you?'

'We can look after ourselves, can't we, Aladdin?'

replied the Child. He certainly seemed his cheeky and confident self.

'I'll be back to get you,' I said. 'I promise.'

The Child looked at me with his large eyes.

'Of course you will,' he said simply. Aladdin whinnied and danced a few little steps in the air. She came to me and nuzzled my cheek.

Then they were fading before my eyes. I was back in the room. I turned to Leela, amazed.

'Here we work with the power of thought,' she smiled. 'Thoughts are things. We have learnt to use the power. It is very simple; it only takes practice.'

'I have done it a few times,' I said modestly.

'Of course,' said Leela. 'It was the power that enabled you to get to the Silver City.'

'If only I could see the Wise Man. *My* Wise Man,' I asked.

Leela smiled, and in seconds there he was!

He was standing under a tree combing his beard. He winked at me. He didn't seem in the least surprised to see me.

'I did it!' I shouted. 'I got here.'

'Pshaw,' he said. 'I knew you would.'

'How did you know? It certainly wasn't easy.'

'I never said it would be,' he grinned. 'I hope you're making notes for the book,' he said. And he held up a book. I could see the title: *Travels with a Wise Man.*

'If it's already written, then you know what's going to happen!'

He laughed, 'Oh, I wouldn't say that.'

'What is going to happen?' I begged.

'Now, would I spoil your fun?' he laughed again and

patted my face. 'I'm very proud of you. Good boy.'

I felt about ten years old, and full of love for him.

'When will I see you again?' I begged.

But his image had begun to fade. I was back in the room with Leela.

'That was the Wise Man,' I said, as if she didn't know. He had led me into such unbelievable adventures. I couldn't help thinking grimly of what might lie ahead. Leela brushed my shoulder, as though hitting away the dark thoughts.

'After you've rested, we will explore the city,' she said. She smiled lovingly at me. 'But first rest. You have come a long way.'

She led me to a round room. It was, again, simply furnished. One large bed, beside it a table, and a small cabinet standing against a wall. And through the glass walls, the sparkling sea.

I thanked Leela and she left. I carefully placed the golden globe on the bedside table and sank gratefully onto the very comfortable bed. I wondered again what meaning the globe had for me, and what I had to do with it. I'd think about that later. Now, I'd enjoy the comfort of a bed and the joy of being in the Silver City.

For a moment I lay looking at the sea, but my eyes wouldn't stay open. I slept in peace.

31

MY DAYS IN THE SILVER CITY PASSED TOO QUICKLY. Sometimes now, when I look back, I'm tempted to believe the city was only a dream, and yet I know it wasn't.

Somewhere, in another time, the Silver City exists for those who believe. And if they truly seek, they will find it.

There hasn't been a day since when I haven't longed to return; that I haven't thought of the Wise Men, Leela, and all the dear and beautiful friends I made there. Yet the Wise Man was right. After you leave the Silver City it is not always possible to go back. I've tried many times. It wasn't meant to be. But one day . . . who knows?

It was a place of beauty. There you could not doubt the existence of God. You were continually in the presence of a Universal Intelligence, you knew only love, joy and peace. You were part of the light, it was all around you, it was in everybody.

As the days went by, I knew myself to be growing in the light. It was impossible to think negatively. There was no darkness in the Silver City.

I realised that if there was any darkness in me, I had created it. It came from my little ego with all its unsatisfied wants and desires. The 'Me! Me! Me!' that plagues us all. I realised all the darkness in humanity grew from giving in to this ego, which had no knowledge of what a person could become.

In the Silver City I became what I was meant to be. I recognised my divinity. I was part of God. And I rested in His peace.

Ah? Such peace. Each day was a new beginning.

Here, nobody worked or toiled. They satisfied all their needs by thought alone. They created what they wanted from thought, knowing that the Universe supplies all our needs, if we trust in it.

As the Wise Leader, whom I met again several times and who was called Oliver, told me: 'My son, when you know your Father loves you, and it is his good pleasure to give you His kingdom, what need is there of fear and worry, of toil or hardship? We already have all, we only have to believe.'

Don't fear. Trust. And believe. I remembered the Wise Man's words. How right he had been. I would never fear again. I would always trust. Always believe.

Oliver smiled as he read my thoughts: 'But we must be on guard, my son. The ego can trick us when we least expect it.'

Even though we met often, he still hadn't told me what I was to do. Every time I asked him he smiled and said: 'Be patient. This is your time to rest.'

I had never felt so rested. Slowly, my lovely guide, Leela, taught me to use the power of thought.

She would say, 'What would you like to do today?'

I'd be polite. 'I don't know. Whatever you'd like to do.' But if there was a brief image in my mind—perhaps a boat on the sea, a picnic in the mountains, dinner with new-found friends, she immediately picked it up, and there we were.

Then she would bring me back and again give me the choice, or ask me to take her where she wanted to go.

I would try. Sometimes my vision wasn't bright enough and I only half succeeded. Leela would laugh, and say: 'You must *believe*. Trust.'

Where had I heard that before? So I'd try very hard to trust, and she'd laugh again. 'Don't try so hard. It is all there for you if you want it. Just accept.'

Gradually I came to accept God's goodness. How could you not, in the Silver City? You were part of it and it was part of you.

Every night as I lay down and closed my eyes, to the sound of the sea and the scent of the beautiful perfumes wafting through the air of Leela's magic house, I gave thanks.

Every night, before I closed my eyes, I stared at the flame in the golden globe by my bedside and wondered what I had to do with it, apart from keeping it alight.

The flame had grown brighter since I had come to the Silver City. Brighter and stronger; it hardly wavered in the breeze. It was no ordinary flame, I knew. Once again, I wondered what its purpose was.

Each day dawned in sunlight and joy. I ran down to the beach and swam in the blue, blue water that lapped softly and warmly around me.

One day I met a dolphin swimming there. For a

moment I was frightened but then I knew no harm could come to me in the Silver City.

The dolphin swam close to me and its huge eyes reminded me of my dear Aladdin. Magically, I realised I could read the dolphin's thoughts.

'Let's play!' it said. We swam together, chased each other, ducked each other and splashed about like two innocent children.

Such harmony and warmth came from this gentle creature. When we parted, it said: 'Thank you. Good luck on your journey.'

My journey. What would happen on my return to the Valley of the Lost Souls? I had to admit I was afraid when I thought about it. I shrugged these thoughts away. I could do whatever I had to do. I was sure of that now. There was never ever anything to fear.

Playing with the dolphin had reminded me of the Child and Aladdin. How I longed to see them again. When would I find them, I wondered. I thought: these problems will take care of themselves. I will live in this beautiful moment.

At one of our meetings Oliver said to me: 'Live in the moment, my dear little brother. If you make each moment good, then that moment leads to another, and another. Create good with each moment and you will help bring God's kingdom to earth.'

Every moment in the Silver City was good. I had never felt so happy. I had never experienced such love. I began to think I was falling in love with Leela but she read my thoughts as usual and giggled.

'In the Silver City we seek only spiritual partnerships. It is more important to share a relationship with someone who is on the same spiritual path as you, and to help them, as they help you.'

I knew now that love was universal and although it was good to share your love with a partner, it was first important to learn unconditional love, to give your love to all, as God's children. And to love yourself.

For the first time I realised how important it was to love myself. I looked back on the person I had been—indecisive, full of fear, lacking in confidence and self-esteem—I hadn't liked myself.

How could I not like myself? I was part of God. Of universal love. Of joy, peace, happiness. I was part of God's glorious kingdom. What was there not to like?

I felt I had been born again. I thanked the Wise Man for bringing me to the Silver City. I wondered when he would turn up in my life again. I missed him.

The days went by. Time did not exist there in our terms. I have no idea how long I lived in the Silver City. I could have stayed forever. But that was not to be.

One morning, when I returned from my swim, Leela told me that Oliver wanted to see me. As I was about to leave the house she brought the flame to me.

'You must take this with you,' she said.

And I knew in my heart that the time had come for me to leave the Silver City.

32

Once again I entered the Great Hall. I walked steadily down the aisle, carrying the flame in the globe.

The Wise Men were assembled on the dais. They smiled, welcoming me as an old friend. I smiled back nervously and knelt in front of them. Leela knelt beside me.

Oliver stepped forward and patted my head, motioning me to stand.

'The time has come for you to leave here, my son.' I nodded, my heart sinking. He smiled kindly. 'But you already knew that.'

'Yes, Oliver. I don't want to leave,' I couldn't help saying. My voice sounded small, like a child's.

'This was only a resting place for you, so you could gain new strength and fulfil your mission.'

'What is my mission?' I asked, and my voice trembled. I was afraid. This is ridiculous, I told myself. There's nothing to be afraid of.

Leela brushed my shoulder gently, as though brushing away my fear. I smiled my thanks, and felt a little better.

'What do I have to do?' I asked Oliver in a stronger voice, determined to put all doubts aside.

Oliver pointed to the flame in the golden globe.

'You must carry that flame to the Valley of the Lost Souls.' There was a sudden nasty jolt in my stomach. 'In the Village there, in the place on the hill, the house of darkness, where the Evil One resides, you are to place the flame in a golden crevice, where it belongs.'

'Where is this place?' I asked.

'You will find it. Once before, the flame of gold was put there but the darkness of the Evil One destroyed it. Now is the time for it to be renewed.'

'Won't he always be able to destroy it?' I said, thinking of the power of the Evil One, who I never really wished to meet again. Oliver sensed my fear, even though I tried to hide it, especially from myself. His voice was gentle, as always, his smile full of love.

'Once you return the flame to its rightful place, darkness will end in the Valley. The souls there will begin to find the light for themselves. As you have found it.'

I stared at him, not knowing what to say.

'Would you deny them that?'

Why me? I thought, very aware that my frightened little ego was once again rearing its ugly head. Oliver, reading my thoughts, answered me.

'Long ago, in another time, you were attached to those souls. You are all part of each other, and only you are strong enough to bring the light back to them.'

I wasn't strong. Leela's hand brushed my shoulder. I took a deep breath. I had come this far, I was not going to fail. If the Wise Men thought I was strong enough, then I must be able to do it.

Oliver said, 'You *can* do this. But you don't have to. If you want to change your mind, no one will judge you.'

'If I changed my mind, would I be able to stay in the Silver City?' Coward, I thought, but I couldn't help asking.

'No. Your time here is over,' he said. I tried not to feel sad.

'I have loved my time here. Thank you.' I said. Oliver smiled his gentle smile, the warmth in his eyes touched my heart.

'It is we who must thank you for reaching the Silver City. For each person who reaches the light, there is rejoicing in heaven. We are very grateful. And we know you will reach the Valley of the Lost Souls. But,' he warned, and his expression was stern, 'you must never let the flame go out. If you do, then you will have failed.'

'I won't fail.' I was surprised how brave I sounded.

'Go then, my son, and God will be with you.'

The Wise Men stepped forward and one by one embraced me. I felt like a hero. Then Oliver and I said a final goodbye.

'Thank you for all the wisdom you've shared with me,' I said. Words were inadequate. How could I ever thank him for the love he, and everybody else in the Silver City, had given me, and for what I had learned there?

'I could not have shared it with you unless you had been ready to hear,' he said. We embraced again. His extraordinary eyes held mine and gave me courage.

'Remember,' he said, 'iron must be forged in the fire before it becomes steel. Go in peace.'

I left the hall of the Wise Men for the last time. Leela walked with me to the gates of the city. All along the streets the people had assembled to cheer me on. I felt again like a medieval hero going off on a crusade.

The crowds followed us to the gates, cheering all the while. Then, as if knowing that Leela and I needed to say our farewells, they drew back and, magically, disappeared as quickly as they had come.

In a moment the streets were deserted, except for the guard stationed at the gate, and he tactfully moved away.

'Goodbye, dear friend.' Leela held out her hand. She had been so wonderful to me. I wanted to hold her in my arms but I was shy. Reading my thoughts, she hugged me and we kissed.

'Will we ever meet again?' I asked.

'We have always known each other. Remember, in reality there is no such thing as time. We are always together. I carry you in my heart.'

'And I carry you in my heart.'

'Don't let the flame go out,' Leela said.

I watched her walk away until she was a tiny figure in the distance. And then finally she was gone.

33

I HAD LEFT THE SILVER CITY BEHIND. ITS SHINING spires gradually faded from view. I reached the crest of a hill, took one last look and silently said goodbye.

I don't know how long I walked. I was forced to move slowly, as I carried the flame in the globe. Despite my good intentions the further away from the city I moved the more I began to feel alone and afraid.

I tried to shrug off my misgivings. When I grew too tired to walk any more I rested. I had to decide what my plan of action would be.

How on earth was I to get back to the Valley of the Lost Souls? Could I just imagine myself there? Should I first return to the crossroads and try to find the Child and Aladdin?

And when I did enter the Village of the Lost Souls, how would I carry the light past the dark force they called the Evil One?

I was depressed. I tried to push my fear away. I'd only been gone from the Silver City for a short time and already I was having doubts. Surely I had learnt enough to overcome doubt and fear?

I looked down at my body. It was much less bright than it had been in the Silver City. I suppose that was to be expected, I thought ruefully, now that I was coming down to earth, as it were.

What worried me more was that the flame in the globe wasn't as strong or as bright as before. When I blew gently on it, it wavered and trembled in the air.

Dear God, I whispered, don't let it go out. I was tired and disgruntled. I wished I was still in the Silver City. My limbs were heavy. I lay down and tried to forget what lay ahead.

I closed my eyes, unable to resist the heaviness that settled over me.

A voice in my ear said sharply: 'Wake up!'

I was so startled to hear the voice of the Wise Man that I was instantly awake. I sat bolt upright.

And there he was, standing in front of me. His dark eyes were not smiling.

'Stay awake, you idiot,' he snapped. 'Don't you realise you carry something precious with you and that if you fall asleep it could be stolen, or worse! It could go out!'

'Wise Man!' I yelled joyfully. I rushed to him and tried to embrace him.

'Pshaw!' He pushed me away. 'Let me look at you.'

'Are you really here?'

'Doesn't it look like I'm here?'

'Yes, well,' I replied, 'it doesn't necessarily follow that you *are* here.'

'You're learning,' he laughed.

'Oh, Wise Man,' I said excitedly, 'I've learnt such a lot.'

'Have you?' he mused. 'We'll see.' Once again he'd put me in my place. It was like old times.

'Well, I think I have.' I tried to sound more humble.

'It's not what we learn. Everybody can learn,' he replied, taking my arm and sitting us under a tree. 'It's putting it into practice. That's the hard part. Then we find out what we've really learnt.'

I wondered if I had learnt enough to get me through what lay ahead? 'I have to go to the Valley of the Lost Souls.'

'I *know* that, dummy,' the Wise Man snapped. 'So why were you asleep?'

'I was tired. Can't I sleep?'

'You carry the flame with you. You can't afford to sleep.'

'But I was so tired!' I said.

'And what do you think made you tired? Your own fear and doubt. Once you allow negativity in, it attracts the very thing you don't want.'

'Does it attract him? The Evil One?'

'Of course!' he said with relish. 'He knows you're on your way. He's just waiting for you to fall asleep so he can blow out the flame.'

'Oh God,' I said.

'Yes, well, if you asked God to help you, instead of doubting, you'd be given the strength not to fall asleep.'

He always knew what to say that would totally squelch you, I thought grimly. The Wise Man laughed as though he'd read my mind.

'He *wants* you to fall asleep, dummy. He'll try every trick in the book to stop you taking the light into the village.'

'Then how can I stop him?' It was hopeless.

The Wise Man looked at me. His eyes gleamed darkly and stared into my soul. 'You stopped him before,' he said simply. 'Don't fear. Trust. And believe.'

I had stopped him before. Perhaps I could do it again. I *would* stop him. I was a different person to the one who had set out on his travels with the Wise Man. I had been to the Silver City. I could do anything, I . . .

'Don't get carried away!' snapped the Wise Man, reading my mind again. 'You've got a long way to go yet. Just stay centred. Calm and centred. And don't fall asleep,' he warned.

'Thank you,' I said humbly. 'I'll try not to.'

'Good. Now let's eat. I'm starving.'

'What do we eat?'

'I don't know, dimwit,' he said irritably. 'You think of something.'

So I did. I thought of some rice and vegetables. And some apple juice. The Wise Man waved his hand and, to my surprise, it appeared.

'We're a good team,' he winked.

Why should I be surprised at anything, I thought. The food was sparse, but it sufficed.

'Mmmm. This is *very* good,' said the Wise Man, eating enthusiastically. At least I'd done something right. Well, with a little help from my friend.

'Now,' he said when we'd finished eating, 'let's talk!'

34

'THE FIRST THING TO DO IS TO REUNITE WITH YOUR friends,' said the Wise Man.

My heart leapt at the thought of seeing Aladdin and the Child again. 'How do I do that?'

'That's up to you. For a start, you could go back to the crossroads and work it out from there.'

'But how do I get them out of that place?' I asked anxiously.

'I'm sure you'll find a way,' he replied, enigmatic as ever. He was not going to be any help at all. I sighed heavily. The flame in the globe wavered.

'How do I get back to the crossroads?' I asked.

'Well, you obviously can't walk back, can you?' he said, pressing me for more answers.

'You mean, I just imagine myself there?'

The Wise Man shrugged. 'Pshaw! Haven't you learnt anything on these travels of yours?'

'They're not *my* travels. You asked me to come along with you.'

'Did I?' he asked innocently, as though he'd forgotten.

'Of course you did,' I said angrily, not letting him get away with it.

'Oh well. I've forgotten. Anyway,' he beamed, 'it's really your adventure now, isn't it?'

And I realised it had become my adventure. The Wise Man had pushed me into it but now I had to do it on my own.

'Will you come with me to the crossroads?' I asked hopefully.

'Oh, I think not,' he said offhandedly.

Of course you won't, I thought bitterly. I'm on my own.

I felt another surge of fear. The flame in the globe wavered. What if I couldn't get my friends out of the Invisible World? What if I didn't have the courage to get the flame into its rightful place in the Village of the Lost Souls?

Old fears flooded back and my stomach churned with anxiety. I felt sick. The flame shook as if it was in a strong wind, and grew smaller.

'What's happening?' I asked, picking up the globe carefully.

'Tut-tut,' said the Wise Man. 'It's your negative thinking.'

He hit my shoulder, as Leela had done, to brush away my negative thoughts—though his touch was a little harder than Leela's.

'You mean the flame is affected by my thoughts?' I asked incredulously.

'Isn't everything? I hoped you would have picked that up by now.'

I stared at the flame. I tried to get control of my thoughts. Does this mean I can't even feel sorry for myself, I wondered miserably. The flame wavered again. The Wise Man laughed.

'That flame is part of you now. It is your light. Don't let it go out.'

I was thoughtful for a long time. The Wise Man was content to share the silence with me. Twilight was falling and I watched the birds flying in and out of the trees. They began chattering and dived happily around the Wise Man's head, as though they knew him. He didn't seem to notice.

Of course, I thought, I must first meet up with Aladdin and the Child. They'd help me to get to the Valley of the Lost Souls. I felt renewed confidence.

'Now, you're talking,' the Wise Man smiled. 'It would be a help to have some company on the way.'

'You could always come yourself!' I said sharply. He raised his hands in a helpless gesture giving me his innocent-child look.

'What possible use could we be to you?'

'Oh come on, Wise Man. You'd be a great help. This isn't an easy task I've got ahead of me.'

'I am always with you, don't you know that yet?' he said, his eyes flaring and piercing mine. There he was looking into the depths of my soul again! He dropped his innocent act and became serious.

'Once a Wise Man has chosen you he holds on to you forever. You and I have been together before and we will be together again. I am always with you.'

'Thank you.' What else could I say? At least his words made me feel a little more secure.

'So. Now we'll talk,' he said.

'I thought that's what we had been doing.'

'No, no. Now we'll talk about important things. There are things I must say before you continue your journey.'

We sat together under the tree and talked long into the night. The Wise Man imparted much wisdom to me, which I'm unable to relate in these pages.

The moon rose high in the sky and still we talked. I didn't notice the time but finally the Wise Man said, 'If you wish to rest, I will stay by your side and keep the flame burning.'

'Are you sure it won't go out if I sleep?'

'I'll watch,' he said.

I thanked him and fell asleep.

35

I SLEPT FITFULLY AND DREAMT THAT I WALKED through the Valley of the Lost Souls and entered the Village, with Aladdin and the Child at my side. The streets were deserted and there was an eerie stillness about the place. It was very dark. The darkness came from a sky heavy with black clouds. It looked as if a storm were approaching but I knew it was the Evil One gathering his forces.

Soon I heard his laughter and the booming voice that was so frightening.

'Fool!' he shouted. 'You really think you can defeat me?'

Lightning bolts lashed out of the sky, striking us. Searing pain went through my body. The lightning hit Aladdin and she collapsed to the ground with a cry.

'No!' I cried. I tried to help her. At the same moment the Child was carried, screaming, away from me on the wind. He disappeared into the oncoming darkness.

'Get up, Aladdin,' I pleaded. 'Please get up!' The horse struggled desperately to move but life was ebbing from her. She could only look at me sorrowfully with her huge sad eyes.

'No!' I sobbed. 'Don't die! I need you!'

The booming laughter began again. I was forced to run for my life, dodging the dreadful lightning bolts, screaming each time one hit me. The pain was intense.

The rain had turned the ground to mud. The mud was like quicksand and as I ran I was tugged down into it.

'Please! Help me!' I screamed.

There was no help. I sank further until the mud was up to my mouth. It covered my face. I struggled for breath, reaching helplessly with my hands, but I couldn't get free.

I sank into oblivion. But then something was shaking me.

'Wake up!' It was the voice of the Wise Man. I opened my eyes. I was hitting at him and kicking wildly.

'Peace, peace,' he whispered gently, holding me still. For a moment I couldn't speak. I was drenched in sweat. My mouth was open and I was gasping like a fish.

The Wise Man put his hand on my heart. I breathed more calmly.

'I had the most awful nightmare!'

'Sssh. It's all right,' he said tenderly.

'Wise Man, I'm so afraid!'

'Sssh . . . ' he stroked my brow. Light came from his hand to my heart. It filled my mind, and my body relaxed. The nightmare began to leave me.

The light in the globe was wavering, dying to a tiny blue flame. Now the flame flared up. I heaved a long sigh of relief.

'It was only a dream,' I told myself.

'This is why you must stay awake. Unless there is someone there to guard you,' the Wise Man warned, 'the

Evil One will try any trick to get into your brain.'

'He certainly got in that time,' I shuddered. 'It was awful.'

'Don't think about it.'

But I couldn't shake a sense of foreboding.

I looked around and realised it was daylight. I stood up and stretched my arms.

'What will we have for breakfast?' I forced myself to sound positive, even though I didn't feel it.

'You're very kind but I can't stay for breakfast,' the Wise Man said.

'You're leaving me now?' I said, my heart sinking again.

'There are things I have to do. I can't spend all my time looking after you.'

'No, of course you can't.' I hated saying goodbye to him.

'Will we meet again?' I asked hesitantly.

'Hmm. That depends,' he said thoughtfully.

'On what?'

'Who knows what will happen.' The Wise Man shrugged philosophically. Really, he was the most irritating man. He smiled again. 'But I'm always with you, remember that.'

He touched my shoulder, as though brushing away the nightmare and any other fears I might be carrying.

'You should be on your way. You have much work to do.'

'Yes.' I didn't move. I had a sinking feeling that this might be the last time I would see him for quite a while. Perhaps *the* last time.

He smiled again, reading my thoughts.

'Now, now! Enough of this silly thinking. You won't have time to think about us, you'll be much too busy.'

'How could I ever not think about you!' I burst out. 'You have given me so much.'

'Oh me. I'm nothing,' he said modestly.

'You are very wise,' I replied.

'Am I? Do you think so?' he asked, playing the simple child again. He beamed as though I had paid him a wonderful compliment.

I couldn't help laughing. He was very beguiling when he wanted to be.

'Don't let the light go out.' He was darkly serious again.

'I won't,' I said firmly.

'Goodbye, my son.' He embraced me. I felt very sad.

'Please,' I begged. 'Will I see you again?'

'If you want to, of course. I am always here.'

If only it were that simple, I thought. He smiled lovingly at me.

'Don't fear. Trust. And believe.'

And then he was gone.

36

I WAS ALONE AGAIN. INSTEAD OF STARTING ON MY journey to the crossroads I sat dejectedly under the tree.

I tried hard to fight my feelings of depression and fear. Half of me, the negative half, didn't want to go on with my quest. I was tired. I wanted to give up and go home and forget I had ever met the Wise Man.

But how could I forget, after all the wisdom he had given me, all the things he had taught me? I could still see his twinkling eyes, still feel his extraordinary presence. Of course I couldn't give up.

As I tortured myself, going back and forth between courage and fear, the flame wavered, growing strong as I was strong, weak as I was weak. I burst out laughing. Here was a barometer of my moods! I didn't dare give up in case the flame went out.

I couldn't let that happen. I would never forgive myself. So, holding the globe carefully, I prepared to return to the crossroads.

I breathed deeply and filled myself with light. I imagined myself back at the four paths. I grimaced and pushed and imagined but nothing happened. I tried again, cursing that I wasn't able to do it! What if I couldn't get back? Don't think like that, I told myself. You have to get back.

I tried again. Nothing happened.

The flame was wavering, getting tiny. Why was it doing that? I was trying to be positive. But I knew a part of me was still afraid and didn't believe I could get back to the crossroads.

The flame didn't lie. It was reflecting my fearful thoughts—the part of me that was afraid to return to the crossroads and didn't want to continue the journey.

I tried to relax. I relaxed every muscle in my body. I pictured the light coming into my body, I felt it, breathed it in, and soon I was smiling because my heart was full of joy.

The flame in the globe was strong and clear. I *believed* I could get back to the crossroads. I knew I was already there if I wanted to be.

I *knew* it, without any doubt or fear.

I closed my eyes and thought of Aladdin and how she began to fly when she needed to.

Now I was going to fly. I was going to fly across time and be reunited with my friends. As I thought happily of this I was transported. In a flash I was back at the crossroads.

There was only one thing wrong. I hadn't brought the globe with me.

I had put it down by my side as I practised filling myself with light and I had transported myself without it.

How could I have been so foolish? I was sweating with fear as I tried to get back to the place I had left. What if someone took the flame? If the Evil One was watching, maybe he had taken it. What on earth would I do then?

My heart was beating madly. I had to control it or my fear would affect the flame. Calming myself, I tried the light trick again and, finally, I was back under the tree. And there was the flame, where I'd left it.

I heaved a sigh of relief. I must never let it leave my side again. I picked it up carefully and, holding it for dear life, I breathed in the light and managed to get back to the crossroads.

It was easier this time. The more I practised with the light the easier it became. It was a good feeling. I wanted to stay in the light. The flame, too, was growing stronger and brighter.

It was hot and still at the crossroads. The sun was high in the sky. About the same hour as when I had left all that time ago. I wondered how long I had been away. Days, weeks, months? I had no idea.

I took the path leading to the Invisible World. It was hardly recognisable. I almost didn't find the path because it was now considerably overgrown. I wasn't at all sure where the Invisible World began, until I bumped into it, and my hand went through.

I jumped back in fright.

Once I got into the Invisible World, could I get out? I had to go in. If I didn't I would never see Aladdin and the Child again. I'd find some way to get out, I would have to, I told the flame as it started to quiver, recognising my fear.

I breathed in, filled myself with light again until I was strong. The flame brightened with me.

Then I stepped into the Invisible World.

37

I FULLY EXPECTED TO BE CLUTCHED AGAIN BY THAT mysterious hand but this time nothing happened. As I finally stepped into the Invisible World a force sucked me through—a force that I was powerless to resist.

I was in a world of lush green valleys and vegetation. Quite different to the arid land on the other side. How was it possible that two worlds could exist side by side? I reminded myself that nothing should surprise me. Anything was possible on this journey I had undertaken.

I turned towards the invisible wall but I couldn't find it. Behind me, where the crossroads had been, stretched more valleys and fields.

I moved forward, expecting to go through to the crossroads, but nothing happened. I walked back and forth trying to cross the invisible barrier.

Well, that's great, I thought. Now I can't get out.

I would think about that later, I told myself, because the flame wavered fearfully. First, I had to find my friends.

I turned around and continued further into the world

in front of me. The landscape was familiar. Surely this was where I'd seen the Child and Aladdin, when Leela had shown them to me in the Silver City?

I reached the top of a hill. There were no houses to be seen, and no people.

'Aladdin? Child?' My voice echoed in the silence. I walked on.

What if I could contact them through thought? I sat still and attempted to picture them as I had last seen them, riding across the hills, then waving and wheeling around towards me.

'Where are you?' I asked. 'I'm here in the Invisible World. Come to me. Show me where you are.'

I tried this for several minutes. I opened my eyes, fully expecting to see them, but they weren't there. Nothing had happened. They'll hear me, I thought. I won't give up. I'll keep on thinking about them and draw them to me.

I resumed walking. 'Don't fear. Trust. And believe,' I said aloud. I laughed as I remembered the Child marching around chanting the words and Aladdin dancing with us and nuzzling my cheek. How I wanted to see them again! I missed them so much.

I walked on, searching for my friends. The sun was hot but all the time there was a cool breeze. Sometimes it touched my face, like a human hand.

I began to experience the feeling of being watched. I looked around but no one was there. Then I heard giggling and laughter. And whispers. I whirled around quickly, sure I was being followed. But again, no one was there.

Ahead of me was a forest that stretched as far as I could see. I entered it and walked into the increasing gloom.

Enormous gnarled trees towered over me, blocking the sky so the sun could barely filter through. It was heavy and very still. A place of whispers and shadows.

I walked quickly, hoping to find some sign of human life. The feeling I was being followed was stronger in the forest. I imagined myself surrounded by eyes. I could hear voices. I wondered if I might be in the presence of the Evil One.

The whispers and the giggles were louder.

'I know you're there,' I shouted. 'Why don't you show yourselves?'

More giggling and whispering. Then silence. I waited, then walked on. I sensed eyes watching me.

I came to a clearing. Through the trees I could see a cabin. I hurried towards it.

There was a boy, about thirteen, waiting outside the cabin. He looked up as I approached. He showed no surprise, almost as if he had been expecting me.

As I drew closer he ran towards me, hesitated, then stopped. He smiled as though he knew me and expected something of me. He seemed oddly familiar.

'I'm so glad to find someone here,' I said. 'You're the first person I've seen. This place seems so deserted.'

'It's not,' he said.

'I'm sure I was being followed through the forest,' I told him.

'There are many people here. You just can't see them. Unless you want to.' He sounded rather terse. I wondered if I'd offended him in some way.

'You mean, they're invisible?' I asked.

'Only to you.' He was very brusque. I'd obviously done something to offend him.

'Of course! I'm sorry. I didn't realise.' I found myself apologising to him and I wasn't sure why. 'I'm looking for some friends of mine—who aren't invisible. A little boy and a white horse. I'm sure you'd remember them if you'd seen them.'

To my surprise, tears rolled down the boy's cheeks.

'Don't you know me?' he said.

'Have we met before?' I asked, puzzled. The boy looked deeply sad. He sat down on the verandah.

'We never gave up waiting for you.'

'We?' I asked.

'Aladdin!' he called.

A white horse appeared around the side of the cabin. It was Aladdin, of that I was sure. But she was so much taller. No longer a young horse. Bigger, stronger, older.

'Is that you, Aladdin?' I asked, amazed. There was no mistaking those huge eyes smiling at me with gentle love as she pressed her face against mine. I threw my arms around her neck.

'Oh, Aladdin, how you've changed. Have I been away so long?' Tears came to my eyes.

'You don't even recognise us,' said the Boy, very sadly. I turned to him.

'You can't be . . . ' I hesitated.

'Of course I am!' he said angrily.

'But you're *years* older,' I said, in disbelief. He nodded. I stared at him trying to see some resemblance to the Child I had left behind. Perhaps in the mouth, around the eyes. This was a teenager. He couldn't be the Child.

Yet, Aladdin had grown older . . . I turned to her. 'Is this the Child?' Aladdin nodded. The Boy was trying to bite back his tears. I'd obviously hurt him deeply.

'I'm sorry,' I said. 'I just can't believe . . . you could change so much . . . '

'You've changed too, you know,' he said reproachfully. 'You look older!'

It was his tone of voice that convinced me. For a moment he sounded just like the little Child I had left behind.

I walked over to him and held out my hand self-consciously. He shook it. We stood looking at each other like a couple of strangers.

Then Aladdin, with a joyous whinny, nudged my back and pushed me into the Boy's arms. And I was hugging and holding him, and hugging Aladdin. And we were all laughing and crying together.

We had found each other.

38

LATER, IN THE CABIN, THE BOY SHOWED ME MY FACE IN a mirror. I did look older. My face was more weatherbeaten. My hair was longer, much longer than when I had left the Silver City. I touched it in surprise. How could it have grown so quickly? I hadn't shaved and instead of a few days' growth I had a beard. I looked a bit like the Wise Man, I thought.

'But I knew it was you,' said the Boy. In my heart, I would always remember him as my inner child, but I could no longer call him that. He was a young man.

Through the window I watched Aladdin. I wondered how old she was. Quite old for a horse, I should imagine. At times she even limped a little.

'Does she ever fly?' I asked. The Boy shook his head.

'She never has again. Sometimes, when I was lonely, I tried to make her fly so we could get back to you. But she wouldn't. I wanted to go to the Silver City, but it wasn't meant to be,' he said sadly. 'Tell me about it.'

As I told about my days in the city, it seemed incredible that I had been away so long. Had I really lived there for years? Time, as we know it, did not exist in the Silver

City. How did it measure in the Invisible World? Was it possible that time went more quickly here?

I asked the Boy how long he thought he'd lived in the Invisible World but he was vague.

'Time seems to just go,' he said. 'I don't feel I've been here very long.'

'You must have been here for years! You've grown up!'

'I know,' he agreed. 'But it doesn't seem very long.'

It puzzled me that he wasn't interested in how long he had been in the Invisible World or that he had grown so much older.

'Tell me more about the Silver City!' he exclaimed.

I began again. The city had already started to seem like a dream. I could almost believe it had never happened. Yet I, too, had grown older.

'How I wish I could go there,' said the Boy, his eyes shining.

'You will one day. If you really want to.'

The Boy was listening intently to something outside the door.

'Come here!' He ran outside and I followed. He was standing with Aladdin by his side.

'They all want to meet you,' he said.

'Who?' I asked, seeing no one.

'Our friends!' He gestured towards an empty space. I heard whispers and giggles.

'Where are they?' I asked.

'Right in front of you.' He pointed again to the empty space. I moved in the direction of the giggles and the whispers.

'I can't see anybody,' I said.

'You will, with practice,' he replied.

Suddenly they were all around me. Hands grabbed and stroked me. I was frightened and backed away.

'Don't be afraid,' said the Boy. There was renewed giggling and laughter. 'They're really very nice. They don't want to frighten you. They just want to get to know you.'

I moved tentatively forward again and allowed the invisible hands to stroke me and touch me. It was an eerie sensation, not unpleasant, like a soft breeze gently caressing my body.

The hands half pulled, half pushed me towards the forest. There were so many of them; I had no power to resist.

'Don't be afraid,' the Boy said again. 'They want you to meet their king.'

'Couldn't I meet him later?' I asked, trying in vain to stop being swept along.

'You'll offend them if you don't.' The Boy and Aladdin followed me. I gave in and allowed myself to be dragged into the forest.

I remembered I had left the flame unattended.

I tried to turn back but I was powerless. I was being carried so fast by the laughing, chattering, invisible people.

We stopped at the clearing I had entered before.

'The flame in the globe!' I called to the Boy behind me. 'Stay with it!'

'Why?' he answered. 'It's quite safe. Nobody will steal it.'

At that moment I saw the globe floating towards me.

'Give me that. Please. It's mine,' I shouted. Borne by invisible hands, the globe floated over my head and out of my reach. There was a lot of loud laughter.

The globe was set down in front of a huge tree. I tried to move to it but the invisible hands held me back.

There was a piercing, unearthly sound. A doorway appeared in the trunk of the tree. A murmur went through the invisible crowd, and then silence.

The Boy knelt down. He motioned me to do the same. I did so, and waited. Then the globe was picked up and held aloft.

'The King asks why you have brought this flame with you,' the Boy said.

'Tell him it is very valuable and I would like it back.'

My heart was beating painfully. The flame wavered, became smaller. Dear God, don't let it go out.

'The King asks why it is so valuable,' said the Boy.

'Tell him that is a secret I can't divulge.'

These people could, after all, be friends of the Evil One. Their interest in the flame made me wonder.

The Boy replied: 'But he wants to know.'

I thought quickly. 'Tell him it is to help heal people. But no one but I must touch it, if it is to do any good.'

The Boy repeated what I had said. There was a pause. Finally, the Boy said, 'The King welcomes you to our land. He says very few people ever find the Invisible World.'

This time I spoke directly to the King and thanked him, though I couldn't see him.

'Could I have the light back?'

There was an awful moment when the light remained with the invisible King and I thought he was going to keep it for himself. But then it was passed back to me.

I held on to it for dear life, promising myself I would not let it out of my sight until I had done what I'd set out to do.

Now it was silent in the clearing. The Boy got to his feet.

'It's all right. They've gone now.'

'I wish I could see them,' I said.

'You will, after you've lived here a while.'

'I don't intend to live here,' I said. 'We have to leave.'

'But we can't leave,' he said, incredulously.

'Why not?' I asked with sinking heart.

'Because, it's impossible.' The Boy stared at me. 'Nobody ever leaves the Invisible World!'

39

'THERE IS NO WAY TO LEAVE,' SAID THE BOY. 'I'VE tried imagining. I've tried walking through the wall. But we couldn't get out.'

For the first time, I examined the Boy closely. I noticed his eyes were glazed. He spoke and moved slowly. He had a haziness about him, a dreamlike quality. I was sure he was under a spell and wondered if he really wanted to leave the Invisible World.

We were back in the cabin, and I told him I had to leave. I was on a quest. I would need his help, and Aladdin's, on my journey.

'Where are you going?' he asked.

He had stayed so long in the Invisible World he had forgotten his promise to help me save the lost souls. I decided not to remind him for the moment. Nor did I explain about the flame in the globe. I would keep that for another time. I didn't want to dwell on the dangers ahead. I would deal with the dangers here, first.

It was enough to get him excited about leaving—and for a moment he was, when I talked of my mysterious quest. His eyes shone at the thought of it. But his interest quickly faded.

'I'd love to go with you. So would Aladdin. It would be wonderful to have another adventure. But it's no use. We can't leave,' he said sadly.

'There must be a way,' I said.

'No, there isn't. We've tried.'

'Do you really want to leave?' I still had a sneaking suspicion he didn't.

He answered reluctantly. 'I'd hate to leave my friends. They've been very kind. And Aladdin's old now. She can't walk very far.'

'They're just excuses. You said you wanted an adventure.'

'I do,' he said, yawning. 'But it's very nice here. Tomorrow I'll take you around and show you everything.'

'You forget I can't see the Invisible World.'

'You'll learn to if you stay here.'

'I don't intend to stay here!' I declared firmly. 'I'm leaving, and you and Aladdin are coming with me!'

'We'll see,' said the Boy, yawning again. 'I'm tired. Let's go to sleep. It's late.'

It was pitch black outside. I'd arrived around midday. Surely I had only been here for a couple of hours? Yet now it was night.

No wonder the Boy and Aladdin had grown older. Time measured differently in the Invisible World. It passed quickly! Much too quickly! No wonder my hair was growing so rapidly. At this rate one would grow old in a very short time! The thought chilled me. I didn't intend to stay and find out.

'Tomorrow morning we're leaving!' The Boy didn't hear. He was already asleep. I was tired myself and felt slightly dazed and dizzy. The magic of this strange place was having its effect on me.

I knew I must not sleep. The flame could go out, or be taken by the invisible people. I stepped out into the night to talk to Aladdin who was standing by the verandah.

'Aladdin?' I whispered, stroking her soft nose. 'I'm sure you could fly us out of here.'

Aladdin pulled away from me as if she didn't like the idea. She, too, was under the spell of the Invisible World.

The night grew on. I was desperately tired. I sat outside on the porch, breathing in the air. I had to stay awake. Now I regretted I hadn't told the Boy the truth. We could have taken it in turns to watch. But I wasn't sure I could trust him to stay awake.

'You'd guard the light if I asked you, wouldn't you, Aladdin?' Aladdin gave a little start. She had been alseep. She trotted over to me.

'I mustn't sleep, Aladdin. Don't let me sleep.'

Aladdin stared at me. I yawned sleepily. At least, if the nights were as short as the days here, I would be all right. It would soon be morning.

But it seemed a long time to dawn. I struggled to keep my eyes open. The flame in the globe by my side was fading. My head fell forward and my eyes closed.

A voice in my ear whispered: 'Where there is light there is no darkness.'

It sounded distinctly like the Wise Man. I sat up with a start, expecting to see him. He wasn't there. But the voice had reminded me to stay in the light.

I shook myself awake, breathed and tried to let in the light. The little flame in the globe grew bright again.

'This is all very well,' I thought, 'but how do I keep the light all the time?' Of course I could keep the light, I told myself! The more I practised the easier it became.

So I sat there in the light until dawn. As I filled myself with its radiance, I filled the Boy and Aladdin with the same light, hoping it would break the spell I was sure they were under.

Then it was morning, and the Boy was wide awake and eager to show me the Invisible World.

'We have to find a way to leave here,' I insisted again.

'Just let me show you the village,' he begged.

'I won't be able to see it!'

'You'll learn,' he said, and taking my hand, led me to Aladdin. We rode over the hill and down into another beautiful valley.

Perhaps it was because time went by so quickly there and it was such a lovely day that I began to feel happy and carefree. Getting to the Valley of the Lost Souls didn't seem quite so important.

The Boy took me to the town of the invisible people. He showed me the spot where it was supposed to be and to my surprise, I could see faint images of houses. The invisible hands stroked my face and held on to me. This time I could almost see them. I was laughing and enjoying myself.

And what a delight it was to ride with dear Aladdin again. She took on my good mood and after we left the village she galloped across the valley like the Aladdin of old.

The Boy laughed delightedly. 'She hasn't had this much energy for a long time.'

If only she would fly, I thought, and take us away from this place. But then it didn't seem so important after all. It was enough just to ride with her and the Boy again. With the wind in our hair, we seemed to sail across the hills.

Aladdin soon wearied. It saddened me to see her lose her energy so quickly. She was no longer young. Before, she would have ridden for hours.

'We'll get her a drink,' said the Boy, as solicitous for her welfare as always. We halted by a stream and Aladdin drank thirstily. The Boy and I swam together and afterwards sat in the sun to dry ourselves.

The Boy produced lunch from his satchel.

'Who gives you your food?' I asked.

'My friends. They look after us well.'

He also took out a bottle of liquid. 'Try this,' he said and handed me a cupful. It was dark, dark ruby red and tasted delicious.

'Mmm. That's wonderful!' I drank it quickly and held the cup out for more. 'What is it?'

The Boy shrugged. 'I don't know. They always give it to me to drink.'

I felt deliciously drowsy. My limbs were heavy. I had to close my eyes. Just a little sleep. The flame in the globe! I forced my eyes open. I tried to speak but the muscles in my throat would hardly work.

'Watch over the light,' I slurred. I tried weakly to reach for the globe but I had no strength. The flame was getting smaller. I had to wake up! I struggled to open my eyes but it was too late. I had no power. I slept.

In my dreams I saw the invisible people clearly. I didn't like what I saw. They had no bodies; they were wraiths with laughing faces. But they didn't laugh with kindness or humour. Their laughter was mocking, mirthless.

They danced around me. I wondered if this was a dream or whether I was in some drugged state.

Then I realised. Of course, the drink! I was not asleep, I was drugged! And as I lay there, day passed into night and night into day and I couldn't move. I could see the light by my side, it was flickering weakly, and what was worse, the Boy was asleep as well.

I tried desperately to reach out for the globe and hold the light close to me but I didn't have the strength. And now one of the laughing wraiths had picked it up, but just as he did, Aladdin bared her teeth at him and he put it down quickly.

Aladdin stood over me, guarding the light from the wraiths. Dear Aladdin. Doing what I'd asked her to, I thought dreamily, as my mind drifted away into some other place. And it was night, and day again and night and then day.

Finally, the effects of the drug wore off and I woke up. The Boy was playing in the stream with Aladdin.

The light was by my side but its flame was very dim.

The Boy saw I was awake and immediately brought me another cup of the red liquid. I hit it out of his hands.

'It's a drug!' I shouted angrily. 'They're keeping you here by giving you drugs!'

'They're not!' he answered defiantly.

'That's why you don't want to leave. If you keep taking this stuff you'll never want to leave! And you'll grow old before your time!' I yelled.

'I don't care,' he yelled back. 'I don't want to leave!' With that he ran off.

Aladdin, torn between us, looked at me helplessly. She started to follow the Boy.

'No, Aladdin! You stay with me!' Reluctantly, she came back. I stroked her face, looking deep into her eyes.

'We have to leave here, Aladdin. But how?'

40

THE FLAME HAD DWINDLED TO A TINY, WEAK LITTLE light. The spell cast by the Invisible World, and by my drinking the red potion, was affecting me, and the flame. There must be a way to leave. There had to be.

I tried to fill myself with light. I was so drugged it was impossible for me to hold the light in my mind. I started to despair, but I shook the fear away. This was not the time to be afraid. I had to be strong.

The little flame looked as weak as I felt.

I tried again to visualise the light but I could think only of sleep. Aladdin watched me curiously.

'If only you would fly, Aladdin!'

Aladdin stared at me as if she didn't understand. She'd always managed to fly before when we were in trouble. We were certainly in trouble now. She must be able to fly again. I was determined I could convince her.

'You can fly, Aladdin!' I took her dear face in my hands. 'Remember? Whenever we needed your help you flew us out of trouble. We need you to help us now. More than we've ever needed it. Please, please fly, Aladdin.'

The horse pulled away nervously.

'She doesn't fly any more. I told you,' said the Boy behind me. He came forward a little shamefacedly. 'I'm sorry. I didn't mean what I said.'

'Then you do want to leave?' I demanded.

'I don't know. I used to think about leaving all the time. But it's so hard.'

'Because you've been drugged!' I pleaded with him. 'I'll tell you why we have to leave,' I said.

I still hadn't reminded him about our quest to save the lost souls. I was waiting until we got out of the Invisible World. Now, I decided to tell him. I had to make him realise how important it was for us to leave.

'Yes?' The Boy waited for me to speak.

'What?' I said, yawning.

'You said you'd tell me why we have to leave.'

'Yes,' I said, and to my horror I couldn't remember. I knew there was something very important I had to tell him but I couldn't remember. It lurked at the edge of my consciousness and wouldn't come through. Not only was I growing old quickly but I was being made to forget . . . I had forgotten already. What? What had I forgotten?

There was a small golden globe at my feet. A tiny flame wavered inside it. It looked as if it would go out at any moment.

'It's to do with the light. The light in the globe!' I said.

'I know *that*,' replied the Boy. 'I knew it had to be important. You carry it everywhere with you.'

'Yes. We must always keep the light with us,' I said.

'You're not making much sense.'

'I can't remember!' I screamed the words. 'I can't

remember what I'm supposed to do with the light!'

'It can't be very important then.'

'It is! It's a matter of life and death!' I grabbed the Boy and shook him angrily. 'Don't you see what's happening? We're forgetting the past! We're forgetting everything! We'll just stay here and grow old quickly. We're trapped.'

The Boy wasn't listening. He was laughing and waving. 'It's not so bad here,' he said.

'Yes! It's beautiful. It's very seductive. But it's not enough . . . we have to get out . . . '

'Here they come,' he smiled. 'They're having a party. Come on.'

'No,' I yawned. 'I'm too tired.'

I had forgotten why I was arguing. I wanted to sleep. Invisible hands stroked me and led me to a tree and laid me down. I closed my eyes.

But a voice in my mind kept repeating: 'Remember the light. Stay awake. Remember the light. Stay awake.' I opened my eyes. Invisible hands had lifted the light up in the air and were taking it away.

Aladdin suddenly reared up on her hind legs and neighed savagely. The hands put the light back where it was.

'It doesn't matter, Aladdin,' I murmured weakly, wondering what I was referring to, and slept again.

41

DAYS BECAME NIGHTS AND NIGHTS BECAME DAYS AND ran in quick succession, like the turning pages of a book.

My dreams were full of the invisible wraiths, dancing around the Boy, and the King emerged from his tree and gave them more of the strange red wine. The boy laughed and fell down asleep, surrounded by his wraith-like friends who caressed him and lay with him.

The King said: 'Bring me the light.' In the dream, I murmured weakly: 'No, no . . . ' Then I would lose hold of my reason for saying no.

Each time anybody approached the flame in the globe, Aladdin frightened them away. She would rear up and kick at them with her front legs. I had never seen her so angry.

'Good girl, Aladdin,' I whispered in my sleep. I knew I should wake up but I couldn't.

And far away in the distance I saw the Wise Man clapping his hands at me angrily and gesturing to me. Then he was whispering into Aladdin's ear. I smiled and thought, 'Who's that funny man?' I was pinched severely.

The pain I felt was very real. The Wise Man pinched me again. I began to surface.

Slowly I awoke. The first face I saw was Aladdin's. She pushed her soft nose against my cheek in relief. The Boy slept soundly beside me.

I managed to stand. I was very weak. I swayed and had to lean against Aladdin to clear my head. I looked down at my feet. There was a flame in a globe. The flame barely flickered. I stared at it and wondered what it was. Something made me pick it up and hold it close to me.

I walked down to the stream, followed by Aladdin. She stood by the globe as I walked into the water and splashed my face with it. I swam for a while and began to feel better.

When I emerged from the water Aladdin was looking at me with big, soulful eyes.

'What? What is it?' I asked.

Aladdin made strange growling noises in her throat. She was trying to talk, to tell me something very important. To my surprise, I could read her mind.

'We must leave here,' she was saying.

'Why should we leave?' I replied. 'It's wonderful, isn't it? Why on earth would we want to leave?'

Aladdin backed away. She was nervous and upset. Again I heard her words: 'Leave. Leave. Before it's too late.'

Then I knew she was right. We had to leave. Yet I couldn't remember why. The effort made me tired and I wanted to sleep.

'We'll think about that later, Aladdin. I'm tired now.'

Aladdin pranced around me, trying to stop me going back to the tree to lie down. I laughed.

'What on earth's the matter with you?'

She became more and more agitated. She pushed me and snarled as if she was going to bite me. I laughed, thinking she was playing, and pushed her away so I could lie down. So she did bite me.

'Ouch!' I yelled. 'Aladdin, that hurt!'

She looked as if she was about to do it again. I edged back to the water, afraid of her for the first time. She followed me, her large eyes dark and menacing.

'What do you want?' I said angrily.

Even as I said it, my anger didn't seem important. I sank to the ground at the edge of the stream. I was still carrying the flame in the globe.

'So tired,' I murmured. 'So very tired . . . '

I closed my eyes. Aladdin made such a ruckus I opened them again. She was desperately prancing around in circles and making high-pitched squealing noises. 'You've remembered you can fly!'

She whinnied and nodded and ran frantically around in little circles, trying to get into the air.

'Fly?' I said, wondering what on earth I could mean. 'You silly thing,' I laughed. 'Horses can't fly.'

This disturbed her even more. She strained every muscle, kicking with her hooves, trying to leap into the air.

'She's trying to fly!' The noise she was making had woken the Boy. He sat up and stared at Aladdin in amazement.

'Horses can't fly,' I said. The Boy's face was a mixture of horror and confusion.

'You don't remember?'

'Remember what?' I said.

He looked so sad. Tears filled his eyes.

'How could you forget *that*?' he said. 'Aladdin did fly. You must remember that?'

'I'm sorry if it upsets you,' I yawned again. 'But it doesn't matter.'

'It does matter!' It was the Boy's turn to shout at me. 'You're right. We are forgetting. And we mustn't. What about the flame? What were you going to tell me about it?'

'What flame?' I asked.

The Boy was obviously upset. He hugged me.

'I don't like you like this. I want to leave.'

'Why would you want to leave?' I murmured. 'It's so beautiful here.'

The Boy spoke to Aladdin. 'You can fly, Aladdin. You remember how, don't you? It's coming back to you.' Aladdin danced around, neighing and whinnying her agreement.

'The light!' The boy said, holding his head. 'I'd forgotten the light! We can get out of here! We'll bring in the light.'

'I don't understand.'

The Boy held up the globe, the flame still burning weakly in it. I took it, staring at it curiously. It had something to do with me, I was sure of that.

'What do you want me to do with this?' I asked.

'Just hold it. Close your eyes. Bring in the light!'

'I don't know what you mean,' I said, yawning. I really wanted to sleep.

'Quick, they're coming,' the Boy whispered urgently, looking in the direction of the forest. 'They know we want to leave and they'll try and stop us.'

'I don't want to leave,' I said weakly.

'Yes you do! So do I!' said the Boy. He closed his eyes. After a while I felt a warm glow move through my body and light began to fill me. I opened my eyes. I was glowing with the light. So, too, were the Boy and Aladdin.

The sound of the invisible wraiths approaching, stopped. I was sure I could see them backing away. And I saw the Wise Man in my head, smiling at me, and slowly I remembered who I was. I remembered my quest. I knew what the flame in the globe was for.

The little flame grew strong again.

I turned to Aladdin. I knew what we had to do.

'Fly, Aladdin, fly!'

'Fly, Aladdin!' chorused the Boy.

Aladdin stood very still. She stretched every muscle in preparation. The light between the three of us grew into a ball.

'Fly, Aladdin,' I said again.

Still Aladdin didn't move. The light began to fade. I thought fearfully: she can't do it.

'Yes she can!' the Boy answered, reading my mind. 'I know she can.'

He began to chant: 'Don't fear. Trust. And believe.'

I closed my eyes and in my mind I saw Aladdin rise up and soar into the air. She giggled skittishly, her tail waving back and forth, her delicate paws prancing in the air.

I laughed. 'That's it! That's it!' I shouted.

And the Boy yelled, 'She's done it!'

I opened my eyes. Aladdin was floating above our heads.

'Hooray!' The Boy clapped his hands.

We tried to get on her back but she was too far away. She landed and, as we got on, the wraiths rushed forward. Invisible hands stroked us, caressed us, held us.

'Fly, Aladdin,' we yelled.

The invisible hands were trying to pull us off. Aladdin strained every muscle. She couldn't move. It was as if she had forgotten the trick.

'You can do it,' said the Boy, with complete confidence. 'Fly, Aladdin!'

He closed his eyes. I closed mine. The light filled our bodies. The wraiths fell away, screaming in fury. Their voices faded into the distance.

And then we were flying.

We soared up and up into the blue sky. Higher and higher we went, laughing delightedly with sheer happiness as Aladdin stretched her limbs and danced through the air.

42

We had forgotten about the invisible wall.

As Aladdin flew into the sky and left the Invisible World behind, from high above we could see for the first time the two worlds lying side by side, and ahead of us we could see through the invisible wall, to the crossroads.

Aladdin came to an abrupt halt, and we almost fell off. Aladdin tried to go forward again and couldn't. We held on tightly as with little moans, she struggled to move, losing height as she did so.

We sank softly to the ground. The glimpse of the crossroads faded and all we could see were the valleys of the Invisible World stretching before us.

We had hit the wall.

'What do we do?' said the Boy.

'We go through!'

I was determined. The exhilaration of flying again with Aladdin had renewed my strength. The further we got from the Invisible World the better my memory became, and with it my energy. The flame in the globe grew brighter.

'We believed we could fly again,' I said. 'We'll believe we can go through the wall.'

'We'll just pretend it's not there' said the Boy.

'We won't pretend. We'll *know* it's not there.'

So we closed our eyes and drew in the light. And when we had surrounded ourselves with the powerful golden glow we moved to the wall.

I pushed my hand against it. It went through to the other side. Holding the globe carefully, I stepped out to the crossroads, leading Aladdin behind me. I turned back for the Boy. He wasn't there.

'Come on! Quickly!' I called. No answer. I remembered you couldn't hear through the invisible wall. But I could feel his fear. So could Aladdin. She jumped around nervously, trying to talk.

'I know, Aladdin. He's frightened. He's tried so many times before to get through, now he doesn't believe he can do it.'

And I could see the Boy in my mind's eye, standing before the invisible curtain. He was desolate. Tears were streaming down his cheeks, he was pushing and straining but he was not getting through.

'Don't fear. Trust. And believe!' I shouted. And I did. I knew without any doubt he could get through. Aladdin and I kept the light with us. I saw the Boy joining us. We embraced him. I was smiling and full of joy.

The Boy ran into my arms.

'We've done it!' I shouted.

'It was easy!' laughed the Boy, and we hugged each other again and danced around Aladdin.

'Thank you, thank you, dear Aladdin.'

Aladdin tried to share our excitement but she was exhausted. Her brow was hot and her coat glistened with sweat.

I had hoped that once we left the Invisible World we would look as we had before. It was not to be.

The Boy's appearance hadn't changed. I still had a beard and long hair. And our poor horse was old, and very, very tired from the effort of saving our lives.

I stroked her soft brow. She nuzzled my cheek and stared at me wearily, her large eyes reflecting the blue of the sky.

'Thank you for reminding me who I was, Aladdin,' I whispered. She nodded, and I held her tenderly for a long time, trying to heal her with my touch.

'Where do we go now?' asked the Boy.

'Aladdin needs to rest a while,' I said, 'before we go to the Valley of the Lost Souls.'

And, of course, now I could remember my quest. I trembled at how close I had come to forgetting it. I clutched the golden globe to my heart. The flame was burning brightly.

'Do we have to go to the Valley of the Lost Souls?' The Boy, too, could remember but he didn't look happy about it.

'We'll talk about it later. Where should we go to rest?'

'I'd like to go to Louise,' the Boy said. 'I'm sure she'd want us to visit her again.'

We sat down, drew in the light and in no time we were standing outside Louise's little cottage.

We left Aladdin nibbling some grass and we walked up the path. I was about to knock when the door opened and Louise was standing there.

'Well, you took your time,' she said crossly, sounding exactly like the Wise Man.

We entered the house. In the kitchen, the table was laid and delicious aromas came from a pot on the stove.

'Sit down! Sit down!' Louise bustled to the stove. 'Don't let it get cold.'

I wanted to ask how she knew we were on our way when we ourselves hadn't known until a moment ago. I decided not to. Nothing really surprised me any more. The Boy winked at me.

'I told you she wanted us to visit.'

After we had said grace, and thanked God and the Wise Man for saving us, we had some of Louise's delicious soup. We ate silently, gobbling it up, for we were ravenous. Louise watched over us like a mother, urging us on, bringing us baked bread that melted in the mouth, pouring strong delicious-tasting tea, and finally she sat down and watched us enjoy the meal.

'When did you last see the Wise Man?' I asked.

'You've just missed him,' she said.

'Oh no!' I groaned. Surely if Louise knew we were coming, the Wise Man must have known too. After all, he had appeared to me in my drugged dream. He'd even pinched me to wake me up!

He had told me he would always be with me. He had certainly tried to help me in the Invisible World. Again I thanked him under my breath, and I thanked God for rescuing us. I shuddered at how close I had come to losing everything. It would have been so easy to have stayed in the Invisible World.

'Is the Wise Man coming back?' asked the Boy hopefully. Louise shrugged, looking exactly like the Wise Man.

'Who knows?' she said. 'He comes and goes. He always turns up when you least expect it.'

Didn't we know it! All the same, I was sad he hadn't stayed to see us. We could have done with some of his advice and wisdom before we began the final stages of our great adventure.

Of course, I knew it was probably intended that we go it alone. Not alone, I reminded myself—he was always with us. Even though we couldn't see him!

'So tell me,' said Louise, 'where have you been and what have you done?'

The Boy and I, between us, filled her in on our adventures.

I decided it was time to tell the Boy what I had in mind, now we had escaped from the Invisible World. We were to journey into the Valley of the Lost Souls, then enter the Village, and put the golden globe back where it belonged.

The Boy went a little pale.

'How can we possibly fight the Evil One?' His voice quavered.

'We have to,' I said. Seeing the look in his eyes, I corrected myself: 'At least, *I* have to.'

I waited for him to say something but he didn't. He sat there looking very frightened.

'Of course,' I said, 'you don't have to come. It would be nice to have help. But I'll understand if you don't want to.'

'I'll leave you to work that out between you,' said Louise, getting up from the table. 'I'll give Aladdin a good scrub down. She looks like she needs it.'

She left us alone. The Boy couldn't meet my eyes. He

stared at his plate. He's not coming with me, I thought despairingly.

'You don't have to decide now. Sleep on it.' I forced myself to smile. He nodded solemnly.

'I'll go and help Louise,' he said. I was left alone.

And I'll be alone, I thought bitterly. Why on earth had I expected the Boy would want to come with me? Even though he had made me a promise when we first set out, of course I shouldn't hold him to it. The journey into the Valley of the Lost Souls would be far too dangerous. How could I expect him to risk his life?

No, I would do what I had to do alone.

The thought of it made me very afraid. The flame in the globe wavered and grew small, and I sank into gloom.

43

It was wonderful to lie in crisp clean sheets again in the cosy little bedroom in Louise's house.

I didn't dare sleep for fear of letting the flame go out. I lay staring at the ceiling, breathing deeply and trying to get into a meditative state so I could rest my body.

The Boy watched me from the other bed.

'Aren't you going to sleep?' he asked.

'I can't. Unless there is someone to guard the flame.'

'I'll guard it for you!' He leapt out of bed. 'I've had enough sleep in the Invisible World to last me years. You sleep. I'll watch the light.'

Since our supper conversation we had avoided being alone together. The Boy and Louise had scrubbed Aladdin down and then he had helped her clean up in the kitchen.

I had gone for a walk and thought about what I had asked the Boy. I was more and more convinced he shouldn't come with me on such a perilous journey.

Then I remembered the Wise Man's words: 'You'll need help along the way.'

In going back to rescue Aladdin and the Boy, I had

almost become lost. It was my friends who had been awake enough to save *me*. I hated going without the Boy. Yet, if he didn't want to come I wouldn't force him.

Now, as he offered to stand guard for me, I realised how much I loved him and needed him. I wanted to ask his decision but I knew I had to wait till morning.

I thanked him gratefully for his offer and closed my eyes.

'Just for a few minutes,' I murmured and sank into a deep, deep sleep.

In my dream, I left my body. The Boy was sitting at the window looking out into the night. He was very thoughtful. Beside him the flame burned bright and steady.

My heart went out to him. I knew he was thinking about his painful decision and what answer he would give me in the morning.

I looked down at my body on the bed. I was again shocked at the difference in my appearance. I was older, thinner, but I looked stronger and fitter than I had ever been.

An inner prompting told me to leave the bedroom and go downstairs.

There, sitting in a pool of light, was the Wise Man.

He smiled and motioned me to sit with him.

'Well,' he said. 'How nice to see you.'

I sat opposite him, and smiled too. We beamed at each other.

'So you got them out okay,' he said.

'Only just,' I replied. 'Thank you for coming to help.'

'Oh pshaw,' he shrugged. 'We can't do much. It's always up to you, finally.'

'Wise Man,' I said. 'I'm afraid.'

'Ssh,' he whispered. 'Don't let the flame go out.'

'I've got to admit I'm afraid sometimes,' I answered irritably.

'Why?' he said. 'God is always with you.'

'I almost lost the light in the Invisible World.'

'Oh pshaw!' he said again. 'But you didn't, did you? You ought to be proud of yourself instead of wasting time thinking about what you might have done. We're all God's children, you know. We're all sparks of Divinity.'

As I talked with him I began to feel light and happy and strong. Whenever I was with him I was sure I could do anything.

'Oh, by the way,' he said, reading my mind again, 'I want you to do something for me.'

'What's that?' I asked, thinking that I was already doing quite a lot.

'I want you to call on one of my friends when you reach the Valley of the Lost Souls, before you enter the Village!'

'Where is this friend?'

'Oh, you'll find him. Just ask along the way, as you approach the outskirts.'

'Who do I ask for?' I said, bewildered. The Wise Man was being infuriatingly enigmatic. Was this another one of his tricks?

'Remember the old man you met in the Village of the Lost Souls?'

'That was you . . . wasn't it?'

'No, no, no. We can't become other people.'

'But I saw you put on his body . . . '

'Did you?' he asked innocently. 'Anyway,' he continued,' I want you to talk to him before you go into the Village.'

'All right.' I was now totally bewildered. And quite sure he was up to something that he wasn't telling me.

'I don't think I should take the Boy or Aladdin. It will be too dangerous.'

'That's up to you,' he said.

'No, it's up to the Boy! He mightn't want to go. I don't think he does.'

'Yes, you're right. It might be dangerous.'

'Yes,' I agreed, my heart sinking again.

'On the other hand,' continued the Wise Man, 'you might need help.' Really, he was infuriating.

'You mean I should take him with me?'

'Oh, I don't know. It's up to you.' He smiled his most beguiling smile. 'You don't need me to make your decisions for you. You're doing very well on your own.'

But I don't want to be on my own, I thought. Then I realised that I *had* made some very big decisions along the way, and I had survived. I was much stronger than before. The Wise Man had taught me self-reliance.

'What do I say to the old man?' I asked.

'Oh, he'll tell you what to do. Don't worry about it.'

The Wise Man beamed at me again.

'Never take counsel of your fears. Remember the light. Keep it burning. Where there is light there can be no darkness.'

Those were his final words as he faded from my vision.

I returned with a sharp bump into my body on the bed. The jolt woke me up. The Boy was leaning over me, his face concerned.

'You were talking in your sleep.'

'Was I?' I replied innocently. I yawned and sat up. 'Thanks for watching over me. Why don't you try and get some rest?'

'I've been thinking,' said the Boy. He was very serious. I waited for him to go on. My heart was beating rapidly.

'I want to go with you.'

'You're sure?' Inwardly I shouted for joy.

'I made you a promise, didn't I? Long ago, when we first set out. I remember now.'

'I won't keep you to your promise,' I said.

'Well, I'm not sure you can do it on your own,' the Boy grinned. 'You'll need me.'

The cheeky thing, I thought, my ego a little hurt.

'Anyway, I was talking to the Wise Man while you were asleep.'

'What do you mean?' I asked incredulously.

'He was here. In this room. He told me lots of things. And after I'd talked with him I felt I really should go with you.'

I fell back on the bed. Now the Wise Man was in two places at once! Why should I be surprised, I thought, and laughed helplessly.

'What's so funny?' asked the Boy.

'Nothing. I'm laughing at myself.' I looked at him seriously. 'I was so afraid you wouldn't want to go with me.'

'How could I let you down? After all we've been through?'

He stuck out his hand.

'Partners,' he said.

'Partners,' I replied, thanking God and the Wise Man under my breath.

44

AND SO, THE FINAL CHAPTER OF OUR GREAT adventure began.

Louise gave us a hearty breakfast. The Boy and I didn't talk. It was not so much that we were afraid of what lay ahead, we were just screwing up our courage.

Louise watched us, her eyes twinkling.

'You're both very serious this morning.'

'We've got a lot of work to do,' said the Boy solemnly.

'Pshaw!' she said. We wanted to giggle; at times she was so much like the Wise Man. 'What's the point of being serious about it? We know you're serious otherwise you wouldn't be doing it. But you might as well be happy while you're doing it.'

Happy, I thought. I'll be happy when all this is over. Louise laughed at my pained expression.

'He always looks so pained, doesn't he?' she said to the Boy, who laughed too.

'Now, now,' Louise told him, her eyes twinkling. 'We mustn't judge.'

Pained? I thought. I don't look pained. I realised the muscles of my face were screwed up tightly into a very pained expression. I immediately relaxed them and couldn't help laughing. We all laughed and felt a whole lot better.

We thanked Louise after breakfast and she said goodbye to us at the gate. She gave us some sandwiches and a tiny capsule of dark green liquid.

'This is to give you energy and strength,' she said. 'Keep it with you and drink it only when you really need it. When you feel you can't go on any more. It's my own special recipe. It packs a punch, I can tell you.' She smiled. 'But perhaps you won't need it. If you keep the light with you.'

We thanked her again for her hospitality, and the Boy hugged her. She was overcome with embarrassment.

'Oh, go away with you,' she said.

I laughed and hugged her too. She actually blushed, her cheeks a bright crimson.

'Go on with you, I tell you,' she said, hitting me away. She patted Aladdin to hide her embarrassment, and Aladdin nuzzled her cheek.

So we set off.

'Always keep the light with you,' Louise called after us. We turned back to wave to her. This time the little cottage hadn't faded from view. It was still there, as was Louise, waving, beaming at us and giving us courage. We waved to her until she was a tiny figure in the distance.

After that, we walked in silence. I noticed Aladdin was limping. 'What's the matter, Aladdin?' When I tried to touch her foot she pulled away. Again, I realised sadly how the years in the Invisible World had aged her. Perhaps her last efforts to save us had been too much for her.

This sort of thinking wasn't doing any good. I turned to the Boy.

'Now,' I said, 'first of all we must try and heal Aladdin. And Louise was right. If we are going to do this, we might as well be happy about it. So we'll meditate before we go any further. We'll see Aladdin healed and we'll see this journey successful. We'll see ourselves achieving our goals easily and effortlessly. All right?'

The Boy agreed. So we drew in the light and saw Aladdin better. We filled her with the light. I felt a surge of confidence and I believed she was healed.

I heard a little whinny and I opened my eyes. Aladdin was floating above our heads. She was prancing about, showing off.

She landed gently and proudly strutted around, demonstrating she was better. Her limp was gone. She playfully butted her head against us.

'Good girl, Aladdin,' I said, stroking her face.

We filled ourselves with so much light that the three of us became a golden, glowing ball. I felt ecstatic and I knew we would triumph on our mission.

I saw the flame in the globe, once again back where it belonged.

I saw myself alone in an underground cavern and I carried the flame with me. In front of me, built into a rock wall, was an alcove with a small grilled iron door.

As I approached it, the door opened and the alcove glowed with a golden light. I placed the globe in the alcove, then I closed the iron grille and it locked into place.

The flame grew bright, its light filled the cavern and I was one with the light.

I opened my eyes.

'Did you see that?' I asked the Boy.

'The light, you mean?'

'I was in an underground cavern and I saw where I had to put the flame!'

The boy shook his head. 'I could only see light. Everywhere,' he said. 'And I was part of it—we all were.'

'We can do this,' I said.

'We *can*!' he agreed.

'Can't we, Aladdin?' I asked. Aladdin neighed and danced around us.

'Don't fear. Trust. And believe!' the Boy chanted, dancing around Aladdin. I joined them. We danced along our way, chanting and laughing until finally we came to the top of a hill. Below us was the Valley of the Lost Souls.

45

THE VALLEY OF THE LOST SOULS STRETCHED BEFORE us once again, lush and green. The sun was shining and everything was still. We could see in the distance the pretty little medieval Village, with its quaint houses and cobbled streets.

Looking at such calm beauty it was hard to believe that this was a place of lost souls. But then, the Evil One wasn't around at the moment. Or was he, I thought uneasily.

'Well, here goes,' I said, taking a deep breath, and we began to make our way down.

'Do you think he knows we're coming?' the Boy whispered. He had read my mind. We looked around warily.

It occurred to me that the pretty picture we were seeing before us was too normal, too calm and much too still. There wasn't even a breeze in the air. It was like the calm before a storm.

As if to prove me right, Aladdin tossed her head and whinnied. She kept looking behind nervously, her ears pricking up.

'What's that noise?' said the Boy. 'Listen.'

At first I could hear nothing. Then in the distance, a piercing whistle, the sound coming closer.

'Look!' said the Boy. Behind us was an enormous black cloud. It blotted out the sun, and moved quickly across the sky towards us. The noise we could hear was the wind of the approaching storm.

'We have to get to shelter!' I yelled. We were in an open field. We ran as fast as we could across the field and down a path towards the houses in the valley.

We didn't get far. The sky above us grew dark. We looked up to see the black cloud had overshadowed us. And with it came the storm. Wind howled around us. It was so furious it whipped up the dust from the path, stinging our eyes and blinding us.

'Lie down on the ground!' I pushed the Boy down and covered him with my body. With one hand I held the flame in the globe close to my chest and with the other tried helplessly to hold on to Aladdin. The poor horse rocked back and forth but stood firm with her head bowed against the awful wind.

And then the voice started.

'Welcome,' it said.

There was a loud crash of thunder. A flash of lightning hit the ground where we lay and danced around us, lighting up the landscape and showing the Evil One where we were.

Another flash. This time the lightning stung. Electricity surged dangerously through my body. I screamed and felt the Boy shudder. I thought I was going to pass out. Aladdin screamed too. She leapt around, bucking her head and kicking her legs, trying to get rid of the pain. There was nothing I could do to help her. I was holding on to the globe for dear life. The little flame flickered from side to side, tossed by the wind. I put my hand over the globe to protect it.

The awful, booming laugh echoed around us.

'This time you won't leave the valley alive!' the voice shrieked with laughter. Aladdin reared up, terrified. Rain poured on us, drenching us. I clutched the globe closer, dreadfully afraid the flame would go out.

The path we were on became a torrent of mud. We began to slide down the hill, losing control because there was nothing to hold on to. Aladdin screamed again and fell to her knees. I tried to get to her but couldn't. I dared not let go of the globe.

The mud swirled around Aladdin and she sank into it up to her knees. It was sucking her down like quicksand.

I couldn't get back to her. I was carried further away. The Boy rolled against me and we tumbled down the hill, swept along by the violent torrent of mud.

Over and over we rolled. Sinking into the mud, then being thrown out of it. Falling into each other, clutching on, then losing hold again. Over and over. I was choking. I couldn't breathe. Mud in my eyes, down my throat. And still, I held the globe to my heart. I chanted: 'Don't fear. Trust. And believe.' Over and over, down the hill.

We collided with a bush. It stopped our fall. We lay against it, panting, heaving, choking, as the mud rose up around us, threatening to drown us.

I held the flame against my chest. It was so very tiny. Barely flickering. I couldn't let it go out. I tried to be calm and get control of my breathing. I heaved a sigh, spat the mud out and closed my eyes. I centred myself, I saw the light growing and spreading through my body.

Soon my body was all light. Then I spread the light to the Boy—and to Aladdin. I spread it around us and through the storm. I saw it move the storm away.

I didn't strain. I didn't push. I rested in the light and let it do its work. I remembered the Wise Man's words: 'Where there is light, there can be no darkness.'

And slowly the storm disappeared. The wind calmed, the rain and thunder stopped. A small sliver of sun appeared through white clouds.

I laughed joyously as I struggled out of the mud.

'We did it. We pushed it away!'

I helped the Boy to his feet.

'Aladdin?' he called, and slipped and slid up the hill towards where we had left Aladdin. She was nowhere to be seen.

'Aladdin!' he screamed.

He tore at the mud where she had been. I ran to help. Then we heard a little whinny and looked up to see a very dirty Aladdin dancing in the air behind us.

She dropped to her feet, treading daintily in the mud. The boy cried with relief as he threw his arms around her neck.

'Oh, Aladdin, I thought we'd lost you!'

Aladdin's eyes gleamed triumphantly, as if to say, you won't lose me. They were the colour of gold. The Boy and I held her tightly.

'We beat him!' I yelled. Then we danced around, throwing mud at each other.

The Boy stopped after a moment, looking serious.

'What's the matter?' I asked.

‘I don’t think we should be too confident, yet,’ he said. ‘We’ve a long way to go.’

That sobered me. We did have a long way to go. A very long way. Yes, we had won this round. But I had a feeling it was only the beginning.

46

We wanted to rest but I thought it better to keep going and try to reach the outskirts of the Village, where we expected to encounter the old man, the Wise Man's friend.

We were a battered trio. Dishevelled, sticky, covered in mud. The sun was shining again and at least it dried us, though we longed for somewhere to wash.

I remembered seeing a lake before, on our way into the Village. We trudged on, hoping to reach it. We walked in silence. Our bodies were so tired from the beating we had received that we didn't even have the energy to talk. As the sun got hotter our clothes were wet again with sweat and our steps were leaden.

'I've got to stop for a minute,' the Boy gasped, and immediately sank to the ground. I sank beside him.

'If only we had something to drink.' He swallowed, his mouth dry. 'I can still taste mud.'

'I know.' I could taste mud, feel mud, smell mud. Aladdin, our beautiful white horse, was almost black. She looked as weary as we felt.

'Let's eat the sandwiches Louise gave us,' I suggested.

The Boy pulled the sandwiches out of his satchel. They were crushed and covered in mud. Impossible to eat. We looked sadly at each other.

'What about Louise's remedy?' Excitedly, I took the tiny capsule of dark green liquid from my pocket.

'But,' said the Boy, 'that's only to be used when we can't go on any more!'

'Well?' I answered.

'Only when we really need it, she said.' He was being very pompous, I thought.

'We need it!' I said. 'We've been through a lot.'

'We might have to go through a lot more.' Really, he was being a voice of doom.

'Then we have the light! Where's your faith? I think we should drink this now!'

I started to open the tiny bottle.

'There's not very much there!' the Boy warned. 'Use it now and you won't have any left for next time!'

'We need it now!' I repeated.

'I've had enough rest.' The Boy quickly got to his feet. 'Let's get going to the lake. We'll keep Louise's remedy for later,' he said, as if he hadn't heard me.

'No!' I said.

I wondered if I was being so argumentative because the Boy was disagreeing with me. But I was sure we should use the liquid now. We needed new energy to go on. We'd been through a lot.

'I wish you'd listen to me for once,' said the Boy, rather sulkily.

'I always listen to you,' I said cheerily and sipped the dark green liquid. I immediately felt better. I could feel the energy surging through me.

'This is great! Want some, Aladdin?'

I gave her some. Her head lifted, her eyes sparkled and took on the green colour of the liquid. She shook herself thoroughly, as though to rid herself of her lethargy.

'You see?' I offered the Boy what remained in the bottle. There was just enough for him.

He sighed. 'Perhaps you're right.' He drank it reluctantly. I knew it was doing him good. I could almost see the energy pulsating through his body.

'Thank you, Louise,' I said, throwing away the bottle.

'Thank you, Louise,' the Boy whispered, but couldn't help adding: 'I'm sorry we didn't make it last.' I gave him a playful cuff around the ears.

'Let's get going,' I said.

With new energy in our step and great good spirits, we set off. It wasn't long before, in answer to our prayers, we came upon the lake.

'Let's have a swim and wash off.' I ran to the edge and was about to go in but the Boy hesitated.

'It might be dangerous.'

I stared at the water. He was right, I thought, remembering my previous encounter with the dragon. But the water was crystal clear and looked so inviting. And I was so dirty. I'd take the risk.

'I'm sure it's all right,' I said, putting the flame in the globe, down on the shore. The flame wavered and looked slightly pale.

I gingerly walked in a few steps. The water didn't seem very deep.

'Come on in! It's fine.'

'No, no. I'll stay here and look after the light,' said the Boy, still frightened. 'Be careful,' he said.

I didn't venture very far. I washed the mud off my clothes, then swam a little way out. The water was cool and refreshing. I put my feet down and found I could just touch the bottom.

'It's beautiful,' I called, before something grabbed my foot.

Large, sharp teeth bit into my ankle and a powerful force started to pull me out into the middle of the lake. I screamed.

'Help!'

The Boy ran into the water. He took my hand and tried to pull me back to shore but he didn't have the strength. I felt as if I'd stepped into a steel trap and I had no power to free myself.

The Boy was losing his grip. He screamed for Aladdin. The horse galloped into the water. She bared her teeth and took a great bite of the Boy's shirt. She tried to drag him back as he in turn tried to drag me. But the creature that had hold of my leg was stronger than both of them.

'Hit the water with your hands,' a voice yelled.

I looked up to see the Wise Man's friend, the old man, standing on the shore.

'Hit the water!' he yelled again.

I bashed the water savagely with my hands. The old man waded in with a large stick and whacked the surface around me.

There was a loud cry of pain from the creature below as it let go of my leg. I swam furiously across the water. In fact, I almost walked upon it, until I stumbled dizzily to safety on the shore.

A huge dragon emerged from the water onto the other bank of the lake. It stopped to glare at me with nasty little eyes before it disappeared into the undergrowth.

'He hates noise,' said the old man. 'It hurts his ears. He's really quite harmless if you stand up to him.'

I stared at the old man curiously. Was he the Wise Man in another guise? He'd been there when we needed him. Perhaps it was the Wise Man. I'd wait and see.

'Thank you for saving me,' I said.

I remembered the Wise Man telling me at the very beginning: 'The dragon represents your fears. Why do you run away from them?' Had this been the same dragon? But then I had only met one. They all looked the same to me.

Did the reappearance of the dragon mean I was still full of fear and not trusting? I had panicked when it grabbed my leg. Who wouldn't, I told myself. I realised guiltily that the low flame in the globe had been a warning. The boy had warned me, too.

'I hate to say I told you so,' said the Boy, right on cue.

'Then don't!' I snapped.

The old man examined my leg. It was bleeding profusely. There was a large hole in it near the ankle, right down to the bone. I felt faint.

'You'd better come to my house,' he said. 'We'll clean the wound.'

'If only we had Louise's medicine now,' sighed the Boy.

'Well, we haven't!' I was tempted to hit him.

'Will you be able to walk?' the old man asked with concern. I was determined to be brave.

'Yes, I'm fine!' I strode on ahead.

'You're sure?' called the Boy. 'That doesn't look too good.'

'I'm all right!' I felt a fool and, not wanting to be treated like an invalid, I walked on, trying not to limp, but I was aware there was no feeling in my leg.

'Do you want this?' called the old man. He held up the flame in the globe.

I had forgotten it again. I was furious with myself.

'I'll look after it,' the Boy said reproachfully.

I heard his words in my ear: 'I wish you'd listen to me!' I thought of the times I hadn't heeded his advice. At the crossroads he had tried to help but I had dismissed him. He had warned me not to go into the lake and I hadn't listened. Was I over-confident and now suffering from the worst of sins: spiritual pride?

The Boy had begged me not to drink the green liquid Louise had given us. If I were able to use it now I might be healed. But I hadn't listened.

Aladdin trotted beside me and nodded her head. She wanted me to ride on her back.

'I'm all right, Aladdin,' I said proudly, even though my leg was hurting. She pulled at my arm.

'Oh, for heaven's sake,' I said pushing her away, 'stop making such a fuss!'

I was immediately sorry I had snapped at her. I'd snapped at the Boy when he had only tried to help. And the old man. I didn't apologise. My mood was too grim.

I strode on, followed by the little troop. I didn't even notice a cottage on the hill as I walked by it furiously.

'No need to go any further,' the old man called to me, 'we're here.'

Feeling foolish, I turned back to the cottage where they were all waiting for me. The old man smiled sarcastically and held the door open. 'After you,' he said.

47

The old man's house was dark and dingy. There was a strange, not unpleasant, musty odour about it. The walls in the living room were lined with books. Most of the subjects were metaphysical, occult or philosophical. It was a most extensive library.

He insisted on examining my ankle. I could no longer pretend it wasn't dripping with blood.

'This will need stitching.'

'Well, I can hardly go to a hospital,' I replied savagely.

'No, no. I can do it,' he said, looking at me sharply. 'If you want.'

I wondered if I could trust him, even though the Wise Man had sent me to him. Was he really the Wise Man playing a role? I was beginning to doubt it. The old man's manner was so brusque and sarcastic that I wondered if he liked me at all.

'Let's try and heal it with the light first,' said the Boy.

Why not use the light and heal it? Better than having stitches. Then I wouldn't have to put my trust in the old man. But as I looked down at the gaping hole in my flesh

I wasn't so sure I could overcome my fear and heal the wound.

The Boy took my hand. 'We can do it,' he said protectively, seeing the doubt in my face.

We closed our eyes. I imagined the foot healed. I saw my leg full of light and the wound closing up.

Slowly, my body began to glow with light. But the fear that I couldn't heal myself kept creeping back. When that happened I lost the light and my body became dark again.

'It's no use. I can't concentrate,' I said.

'You're in the Valley of the Lost Souls,' said the old man. 'It isn't easy to retain the light here. That's why you've been sent to bring it to us.'

I watched the flame in the globe, still so small, and wavering weakly in the air. Please, don't let it go out, I said silently.

'Perhaps you'd rather the stitches,' said the old man, almost as if he was enjoying my fear.

'No!' I replied. 'It'll get better.'

But it didn't. Soon I was in a fever.

I lay on a bed somewhere in the house and tossed and turned. I was soaking wet. I dimly remember the Boy and the old man taking it in turns to wipe my brow. My last thought was for the flame. The Boy had placed the globe by my bed so that I could see it. The flame was so tiny now. I willed it to grow strong again but the fever took over.

Sad, terrible images haunted my dreams. Hands were trying to take the flame; lines of lost souls staggered towards me, pleading, their arms outstretched, and all the time I could hear the laughter of the Evil One . . .

'You won't succeed,' he laughed. 'You? You're nothing. A little weakling. You're not worthy to carry the light.' And in the dream I saw the flame dwindling, dwindling . . .

The Boy stayed with me. Whenever I would drift back into consciousness I could find him sitting by me with his hands on the wound.

'It's better,' he would say. If I attempted to look at the ankle, he would push me back on the bed.

'No, no. It's better. Believe it. Just rest.'

Again, I would try to fill my body and the wound with light. For a while I could do it but then the fear would return. Fear that I should really have had the wound stitched, that I wouldn't get better.

I would lose consciousness again, and as I sank back into the fever, the Boy would murmur in my ear. 'It's better. Don't fear. Trust. And believe.'

Then, in my feverish state, the Wise Man appeared to me. He knelt down beside me and put his hands on my wounded ankle. He smiled and whispered: 'Let go. Let go. God loves you. Let go of fear.'

In my dream, I thanked him and found I could let go of fear and really believe I was better.

It was late into the morning of the next day when I woke. My fever had gone but my leg was throbbing painfully. My eyes focused on the flame in the globe. It was growing stronger.

'How do you feel?' The Boy was still sitting with me.

'Much better,' I said. I didn't want him to know what pain I was in. I wanted to examine the wound but decided not to. Better not to look at it.

I dragged myself off the bed. A searing pain went

through the leg as I put it down. I limped across to the door. Every step was agony. The Boy tried to help me but I pushed him away.

'It's all right. I'm all right.' I forced a smile.

The Boy followed me solicitously as I limped downstairs to find the old man sitting in his study, reading.

'Your leg isn't better?' he asked, watching me limp in.

'Yes, it is!' I clung to the Wise Man's words: 'Let go. Let go.' I tried not to think about it any more and to let go of the pain.

'You've wasted another day,' the old man said, shrugging. He gave me no sympathy at all. 'There isn't much time left, you know.'

'What do you mean?'

'We were expecting you a long time ago. The people waited so long for you but now they don't believe you will come.'

'But they cheered before! "Bring back the gold", they said!' I had gone through so much for these people! Now he was telling me they didn't remember!

'That was long ago! They no longer believe.'

'I have the flame with me, isn't that enough?'

'It is just a light, your light, until it finds its rightful place.'

'But I know where that is!' I said excitedly. 'It's in a cavern, underground somewhere. I saw it in a dream!'

'You still have to find it.' What a depressing old man.

'We'll find it,' said the Boy bravely.

'I hope so.' The old man didn't seem so sure. 'The Evil One will have many traps in store for you. And he is confident, because nobody believes in you any more. It will be very much harder to take the flame to its rightful place if the people do not believe.'

I was shocked. I had been too long in the Invisible World. Because of my foolishness in getting caught up in its spell, I had delayed the quest to take the light to Village of the Lost Souls. And now I had injured myself as well. Really, I was hopeless.

'There's no use cursing yourself,' said the old man, 'that doesn't achieve anything.'

I wondered again if I was really talking to the Wise Man. He could be in two places at once and I had seen him take on the guise of the old man. If so, why was he using this role to talk to me? He would have his reasons. And then, perhaps, this old man *was* who he appeared to be.

'Well?' The old man stared at me impatiently, his manner certainly more brusque than the Wise Man's.

'Well what?' I replied, equally brusque.

'Are you ready to carry the flame into the Village?'

'If it's not too late.' Part of me was hoping it was.

'It almost is, I fear. By delaying so long you have made the task very difficult for yourself. Almost impossible.'

Thanks a lot, I sighed inwardly.

'But,' he continued, 'if you find even one person in the Village to believe that you are the bearer of the flame, then you may find your way to put the golden globe in its rightful place.'

'Just one person?' asked the Boy. 'That's all we need?'

'You'll be very lucky to find one,' said the old man. 'And I warn you. Because the people have lost faith, the power of the Evil One is now enormous. You will have to be very clever to defeat him.'

'Can you tell us how to do that?' I asked.

'With the light. Your belief must be greater than his darkness.'

We were silent. The only sound the ticking of a clock.

'We can defeat him. I know we can,' said the Boy. How brave he was! I could do with a lot more of his courage, I told myself as my leg twinged painfully again. I resolutely saw it getting better, shutting out all thought of pain.

'Yes, we can. And we will,' I said.

The old man smiled kindly for the first time. His stern face looked almost gentle.

'Good. Then I will help you. You must creep into the Village by night. In the darkness it will be easier to hide from the Evil One and his forces. But beware. Do not trust anyone until they prove themselves to you.'

He moved to a cupboard and brought out two black hooded robes.

'I would suggest you wear these.'

We put them on. They fitted exactly. We looked like hooded monks.

'This is what the forces of the Evil One wear.'

'How did you know our size?' I asked, trying not to sound surprised.

'We've been expecting you for a long time.' The old man smiled again.

'Can we take Aladdin?' asked the Boy.

'I would not advise it. You will be less conspicuous on foot. She'll be safe with me.'

Our hearts sank.

'We couldn't leave Aladdin behind!' I said.

'She saved our lives!' the Boy added.

'Then you wouldn't like anything to happen to her.'

The old man's warning terrified me. He knew the power of the Evil One and so did we. Aladdin was old, I reminded myself, she had done enough for us. The old man was right. We would leave her behind. I looked at the Boy sadly. He nodded agreement.

So, when night fell, dressed in our black monks' garb, we said goodbye to Aladdin.

She knew something was wrong. She paced back and forth nervously, nuzzling each of us in turn, refusing to let go. It broke our hearts.

I gently stroked her dear face.

'No, Aladdin. You're to stay here. We'll come back to you.' Aladdin whimpered softly. Her sweet eyes turned dark grey with bewilderment.

'Please understand, Aladdin. It's for the best,' said the Boy stoically, though his eyes were full of tears.

Aladdin couldn't believe we were leaving her behind. She pranced around us, giving little agonised squeals. She blocked our way.

'Aladdin. No!' I tried to be firm. It was hard. She so badly wanted to come with us. 'No, Aladdin. Not this time.'

'We'll come back for you,' the Boy said again. 'I promise.'

Finally, Aladdin bowed her head silently. She stood very still, and sad. But she accepted our decision.

The Boy flung his arms around her.

'I love you, Aladdin.' Tears rolled down his cheeks.

The old man took Aladdin from us and led her back to the gate. We said goodbye and thanked him for his help.

'Don't delay,' he warned. 'Do what you have to do as soon as possible. If you remain in the village for too long you may never get out.'

It was a bright moonlit night. The old man had directed us to a path which led through some woods, from where we could enter the Village without being noticed.

'Hurry through the woods,' he warned us again. 'Dark forces lurk there that would harm you.' My heart took a little leap. He certainly knew how to frighten! But he smiled gently as he waved us off.

'If you keep the light with you, you will be safe.' They were his final words.

As we approached the woods we heard a horse neigh behind us. There on the top of the hill in the moonlight was Aladdin. She stamped and tossed her head and called to us.

'Goodbye, Aladdin,' whispered the Boy.

Then we turned our backs on our friend and went into the darkness of the woods.

48

THE BLACKNESS OF THE WOODS MADE IT ALMOST impossible to see. It was a fearful place, full of strange noises. The old man's warning rang in my ears. I held up the flame in the globe to light the path, and the Boy and I moved stealthily and as quickly as we could. The little flame wavered nervously.

Strange things reached out and touched us in the darkness. Straggling leaves brushed our cheeks, creepers twined themselves around our legs, wet slimy substances stuck to us. We were continually hitting away frantically. Not being able to see made it more frightening. Then worse, for a moment we were caught up in a spider's web and the Boy and I screamed. The terror of the giant spider still stayed with us. How long ago that seemed, and what worse nightmares lay ahead?

The flame wavered furiously, reminding me to guard my thoughts. I took the Boy's hand.

'Take a deep breath, and feel the light. And when we have it, we must try to keep it with us all the time. It's our only hope.'

We stood silently in that dark and sinister place and

brought in the light until our faces shone with its glow. We smiled at each other as the flame grew strong again.

We moved forward, keeping the light in our hearts. Then we heard footsteps behind us. Many footsteps. And voices. Coming closer. We stopped.

The murmuring voices crept nearer.

'Strangers,' they whispered and hissed. We didn't dare move. My heart began to beat faster. I tried to shut out my fear and cling to the light. The little flame in the globe trembled.

Loud cackles of evil laughter floated around us. It was terrifying because we couldn't see anything. The Boy screamed as something suddenly took hold of him and began to pull him away.

I reached out for him but gasped as I bumped into something else—a cold, dank creature whose breath stank and who laughed and tried to hold my arms in its clammy hands.

'Strangers,' it hissed.

I held the globe up to the creature's face. It was a face that still haunts my dreams, and one I never want to see again. A face of such baseness it made me shudder. I glimpsed bloodshot eyes and a toothless smile leering menacingly at me. I backed away, still holding the globe in front of me.

'This is the light that will save the lost souls!' I shouted, desperately hoping one of the creatures would believe me. Or that the light would make them leave.

The dark figures fell back. I heard them running away. The Boy groaned in the darkness. I found him lying on the ground in front of me.

I helped him up. 'Are you all right?'

'I think so.' He was breathing heavily. 'They were horrible.' He took my hand. 'Let's get out of here, quickly!' We moved forward cautiously.

'When I held the flame up to their faces they ran away,' I told him.

'We have to keep the light,' the Boy murmured fiercely.

Again we spread the light before us, with our thoughts, and this time we believed that we were protected. We sensed the dark creatures on either side of us but they didn't bother us again.

And as the light grew stronger it led us out of the woods, and there before us was the Village of the Lost Souls.

The Village was silent and devoid of any signs of life. We crept into it along a deserted street. No street lamps were lit, and there were no lights in any of the houses. Only the moon shone mistily through the clouds.

'What do we do now we're here?' asked the Boy, as our heels clicked eerily on the cobbles.

'Let's stand still and ask for help.' I was becoming more and more inclined to rely on the light. So we stood still and visualised.

I pictured the underground cavern that I had seen before. I saw a stairway led from the cavern and I followed it. I found myself outside an enormous pyramid-shaped building perched at the top of a hill. At the bottom of the hill was a square, surrounded by houses.

'Did you see that?' I asked the Boy.

'It's in some sort of pyramid place.'

'Then we'll find that. Which way, do you think?'

The Boy hesitated, then pointed to the end of the street

where it curved to the right. 'To the right.'

'Okay,' I smiled. 'I trust your judgement.' This time I would listen to him.

We turned right. The street became very narrow and wound steeply upwards. There was still no sign of life. All the houses were dark. We tried to move silently but our footsteps rang on the cobblestones.

'Sssh!' The Boy stood very still, listening intently. 'Listen!'

I heard footsteps behind us. Now they stopped.

'We're being followed,' said the Boy. We walked on further, then stopped. Again we heard the footsteps, and again they stopped.

There was a narrow lane on our left. I pulled the Boy into it and we waited, hardly daring to breathe.

The footsteps edged closer and several dark figures appeared, all wearing the black hooded cloaks.

'The forces of the Evil One!' The Boy spoke in a terrified whisper and I put my hand across his mouth.

The figures moved past. We waited for what seemed a very long time, frozen against a wall, trying not to breathe. When their footsteps had faded away we crept out of the little lane and continued up the street.

The street became very steep, almost perpendicular. I had forgotten about my sore leg but now it was hurting badly.

The Boy noticed I was limping. 'Are you all right?' he asked.

'Yes.' I tried not to think of the pain, and to bring in the light.

Soon we were panting and out of breath. It felt as if we were climbing a mountain. We struggled on wearily.

The throbbing in my leg became worse. I tried to ignore it but every step was agony and each time I placed my foot on the ground, piercing pain went through the ankle. I had to keep stopping. The Boy took my arm and pulled me along.

Exhausted, we finally reached the top and found ourselves in a square. There before us on a hill above the square was the pyramid. Almost as if to show us the way, the moon came out from behind the clouds, and the pyramid was reflected in its silvery light.

Then lights came on all around the pyramid and the street lamps in the square lit up.

Between us and the pyramid were the forces of the Evil One, lined up across the square, waiting for us.

Lights went on in all the houses in the square. Doors opened and people poured out of the tiny houses. Men, women and children surrounded us.

'Imposters!' they shouted. 'Leave the Village. We don't want you here! Imposters!'

We were startled by the vehemence of their attack. I held up the flame in the globe.

'We are not imposters! We have brought this flame to save you.' They fell back in silence. I walked towards them, holding the flame in front of me.

'Here it is. Believe me and you will be saved. This is the flame that will light your way.'

A man in the crowd roared with laughter. 'That little thing? How could that save us?'

The people laughed with him. I moved through the crowd, holding up the flame to each person, trying to find someone who would believe me. They either laughed or turned away.

There was a woman in the crowd with a sweet face. She had a child with her, a little girl with golden hair and blue eyes. The mother stared at me so intently when I held the flame up to her that for a moment I was sure she believed me.

'This is your light. This is what you have waited for. Please believe me.'

The woman shook her head sadly. 'I can't believe any more. It has been too long.' She took the child's hand and walked away. The child looked back at me curiously.

The crowd began to disperse. They weren't angry or mocking now but seemed resigned to their fate. They returned quietly to their houses. I was immeasurably depressed. I had not expected to find such total disbelief.

The Evil One had beaten us without having to do anything. No wonder his forces hadn't moved to attack us, I thought.

But I was wrong. The square was now empty except for the line of hooded men stretched across the street, their faces hidden in the darkness of their hoods. We could see only yellow eyes, gleaming at us. Then they moved in unison, pulling long, thin silver daggers from their sleeves, the daggers glinting in the moonlight.

'Get them!' ordered a voice. They moved silently towards the Boy and me. There was nowhere for us to go but back down the hill we had just climbed. At least it would be easier going down than it had been coming up. We turned and ran.

The hill was so steep that we couldn't keep our footing and I slipped and fell. The Boy tried to save me and he, too, fell. I rolled heavily down the steep slope with the Boy tumbling after me.

We landed with a crash at the bottom. I lay there, still holding onto the globe which, remarkably, hadn't broken. My body hurt terribly and when I tried to move I found I couldn't get up.

I could see the row of hooded figures outlined at the top of the hill. They began to move down the slope.

'Quickly. Get up!' The Boy stood over me. I tried to move but my leg was hurting terribly. I lay back on the ground.

'Please get up. We've got to get away.' The Boy half pulled, half dragged me to my feet. Leaning on his shoulder, I tried to take a step but I was in unbearable pain.

The dark forces were coming down the hill. They were clearly used to the slope and had no trouble retaining their balance. They glided, quickly and silently.

'Take the flame and go,' I begged the Boy.

'No. It's your flame. I can't take it for you.'

'Please!' I shouted. 'Otherwise they'll put it out.'

'No! I'm not leaving you here. Please try to walk!' He attempted to drag me with him but it was no use. I couldn't walk.

The dark forces had almost reached the bottom of the hill. Then, we looked and saw another line of hooded forms in front of us, blocking our way.

We were trapped.

49

'RUN, BOY, RUN,' I WHISPERED AND THRUST THE globe athim. 'Take the flame! If you leave now you'll outrun them! Go!' Without me to hinder him he might have a chance.

'No, I'm not leaving you,' he said.

We stood helplessly as the dark forces on either side approached us, their long daggers raised for the kill.

All I could think was that I had failed. Tears rolled down my cheeks.

'Oh dear God,' I whispered, 'don't let me fail!'

Where are you, Wise Man, I pleaded.

And I heard his words: 'Where there is light there can be no darkness.'

At that moment the Boy shouted: 'Let there be light!'

His voice rang out so powerfully in the silence that he took the hooded monks by surprise. They stopped, and waited.

The Boy closed his eyes and drew in the light. His body glowed. I took the light and we worked until it became a powerful ball which radiated out behind and in front of us.

The dark forces fell back.

'You have no power over us,' I shouted. The light grew and grew until it flooded the streets, and I felt my heart lift. I could no longer feel the pain in my leg, and the flame in the globe was shining brightly.

'Look!' The Boy was pointing up to the sky.

There, in a ball of light, was Aladdin flying towards us, her long legs dancing in the air, her tail waving, her head up, her mane flying.

'Aladdin!' The Boy called joyfully.

Aladdin lowered herself to the street, right in front of us, and we rode with her up into the sky. Up and away from the dark forces who ran after us, shouting and waving their daggers uselessly.

I put my arms around Aladdin's neck and hugged her.

'Thank you, thank you,' I whispered.

'Thank you, Aladdin!' the Boy yelled at the night sky.

Aladdin rose easily over the steep, mountainous hill and into the Village square.

'To the pyramid, Aladdin!' I shouted.

With the breeze in our hair and the stars above us we flew towards the pyramid.

But as we approached, it seemed to move further away.

'Is it really moving?' asked the Boy, in disbelief.

I was sure it was some sort of illusion created by the Evil One. Aladdin stretched through the sky, but we came no closer to the pyramid. The Village square was beneath us but the pyramid was not where it had been before.

Then the lights around the pyramid went out.

In the blackness we couldn't see it at all. Aladdin hesitated and floated softly in the air, waiting for us to tell her what to do.

And then the storm began.

Lightning, thunder, wind! Terrifying, gale-force wind! This was by far the worst storm we had encountered. We were hurled away from the pyramid and tossed helplessly in the air.

Aladdin strained every muscle to move forward but she had no strength against the terrible winds that blew her backwards. The Boy and I held on for dear life, terrified we were going to be blown off and fall to our death in the square below.

The laughter started. The awful laughter of the Evil One.

'This time you're going to die,' said the voice.

Lightning shot through us. Aladdin screamed and we went hurtling downwards.

The ground rose up to meet us. Aladdin fell into the Village square. She was unconscious before she hit the ground. As she smashed onto the cobbled streets the Boy and I were thrown off. Even in those last moments I held on to the globe. By trying to protect it I landed on my bad leg. I felt it snap under me. But that pain was nothing compared to the pain from the lightning bolts that were coming from every direction and burning our bodies.

Rain poured down. It stung as it pounded our faces. Aladdin was lying on her side. I tried to reach her but the lightning struck at me and the rain and the wind tried to push me back.

I felt only anger at what the Evil One had done to us. My anger gave me the strength to crawl through the storm to Aladdin. The Boy was already kneeling by her side. I thought she must be dead, her poor, broken body was so still, but when I touched her I could feel her breathing. She gave a little groan and opened her eyes. She tried to lift her head. The effort was too much. She could only look helplessly at us. Her big sad eyes had no colour; they were blank and filled with tears.

'Oh, Aladdin, I'll save you!' the Boy wept, and put his arms around her. 'I'll give you light.'

Even as he said these words, the wind, with a great venomous howl, picked him up and threw him violently into the sky.

'No!' I yelled. Terrified, I tried to grab hold of him but I had no chance. He disappeared into the heavy torrent of rain. The Boy screamed—a terrible scream that lasted a long time, until it faded away into the tumult of the storm.

Desperately, I tried to make Aladdin get up.

'We have to save him! You've got to fly, Aladdin.' Aladdin could only look at me sadly for a moment, then she closed her eyes. She was hardly breathing.

'Please, please get up, Aladdin!' But I knew she couldn't. My body shook with grief. My tears mingled with the rain.

'We've lost him, Aladdin! We've lost the Boy!' I whispered the words over and over again. I couldn't believe the horror of what had happened. Aladdin whimpered softly.

A figure appeared out of the rain and stood by my side. A woman's voice shouted above the noise of the storm: 'You must come with me!'

'No,' I moaned. 'I won't leave her.'

'You must,' said the woman, 'or you'll be killed.'

I was in shock and could hardly comprehend what she was saying but I knew I would die if I stayed there. The lightning was still darting around me.

The woman's hand reached for mine and helped me up. We pushed against the rain and the wind until we reached the doorway of her house.

When I looked back through the sheets of rain I could no longer see Aladdin.

The woman led me into the house. There, in a cosy little room with a welcoming log fire, I sank into an armchair and sobbed.

'You'll be safe here,' she said kindly, but I hardly heard her. I was too shocked. I had lost the Boy and had left Aladdin to a lonely death in the rain. My heart was broken. I could not go on.

I looked down and saw that I was still clutching the flame in the globe tightly to my heart. Amazingly, the rain hadn't extinguished it, though it was barely alight. At any moment it would die. Its strength was mine and I had no strength left.

A little hand reached out to touch the globe. I looked into two large blue eyes. The little girl with blonde hair, who had stared at me so curiously in the crowd. The woman who had saved me, was her mother.

The child smiled. A sweet, comforting smile. She touched the globe again, her eyes full of wonder.

'I believe,' said the child. 'I believe in the light.'

50

THE MOMENT THE CHILD SPOKE THESE WORDS, THE storm ceased and the flame shone again.

It was very quiet outside. The little girl gently wiped my tears away and then, taking my hand, she led me out into the street.

It was daylight. The sun was shining brightly, as if the storm had never been.

Aladdin lay in the centre of the square. I limped over to her. I felt as if I had broken my ankle. Each step was agony. The little girl held the globe for me as I knelt by Aladdin's side.

She was still alive but her breathing was very faint. At my touch she opened her eyes slightly, as though she had been waiting for me. Now she could die in peace. She made little gasping noises in her throat as if she were trying to tell me.

I couldn't believe I could lose both her and the Boy now, when we had come so far and had finally won the battle against the darkness.

'Oh, Aladdin,' I cried, holding her close, willing her to live. 'You can't die! I won't let you!'

Doors began opening in the square and people came from everywhere. They stood around us silently and shamefacedly.

I held her dear face in my hands. 'Everything will be all right now. We've found one person who believes! We've saved the Lost Souls!'

It was no use. Aladdin struggled for a moment in my arms, making a final effort to stand up. Then she let go. She gave me a last, gentle look. Her body heaved a great, gasping sigh, she closed her eyes and lay still.

'Please don't die!'

I lay across her body and sobbed my heart out.

Yet, above my grief, I could hear a little voice that sounded very much like Aladdin's . . .

'Don't cry,' it said. 'There is no death.'

Then the little girl touched my shoulder. She handed me the flame. My grief must wait. There was one final thing I had to do. The child put out her hand and took mine.

I left Aladdin's side and moved through the crowd. We began to climb the hill towards the pyramid. The crowd cheered.

I limped slowly up the hill. I kept having to stop because of the pain in my leg. The child would wait patiently until I had rested and would then help me to keep going.

I don't know how I took those last faltering steps. My grief at the loss of Aladdin and the Boy was so great, my body so tired and in such pain. I clenched my teeth and muttered over and over again: 'Don't fear. Trust. And believe.'

And the little flame stayed burning brightly.

The pyramid was much closer than it had appeared in the night. The Evil One's illusions had ceased.

At the side of the pyramid an open door led to the staircase, just as I had visualised. The child stopped at the door and withdrew her hand from mine. I knew that I must take these final steps alone, as in my dream.

'Thank you for believing.' I kissed her on the cheek. Then I entered the pyramid.

I walked downstairs to the underground cavern, carrying the flame gently before me. And there, in front of me, was the alcove with the small grilled iron door.

I approached it and the door opened. A crevice glowed with a golden light, as I had been shown.

I carefully placed the flame in the globe where it belonged. I closed the iron grille and it locked into place. The flame grew brighter and stronger until its glow filled the cavern.

The light leapt into my heart and I became one with it. I turned to walk back up the stairs and found my leg was totally healed.

Then there was a blinding flash and I was no longer in the cavern.

The Village of the Lost Souls had vanished. I was standing on an open plain and the Wise Man was walking towards me.

He held out his hand. I took it, and we embraced.

'So,' he said, beaming. 'We did it.'

We, I thought? It seemed to me that I had done it. The Wise Man laughed as though he'd read my mind. I looked around, bewildered.

'What happened to the Village of the Lost Souls?'

'Gone. They're not lost any more. So they've moved on.'

'Oh,' I said. I didn't understand. I didn't understand anything. I was too tired and weary, and how my heart broke when I thought of the Boy and Aladdin.

I sighed deeply. 'I've lost my friends,' I said.

'Oh pshaw.' The Wise Man waved an impatient hand. 'Look!'

I looked up into the sky, and there was Aladdin riding on the wind. She smiled down at me, her tail waving, her long legs striding through the air.

'There is no death,' said the Wise Man.

'Is she a spirit now?' I asked.

'Does she look like a spirit?'

Aladdin certainly looked very much alive as she did a last joyous little dance, kicked her legs and flew away.

'Will I see her again?' I asked, feeling a little hurt that she hadn't come down to talk to me.

'Phsaw,' the Wise Man exclaimed. He was, as always, unperturbed. 'Whenever you want to. You've got a mind, haven't you? Use your imagination.'

'And what about the Boy?' I asked.

'He is part of you. He was the inner child you wouldn't listen to. Once you listened, he was able to grow up. Now you're one.'

'But I want to see him and talk with him.'

'You can talk to him any time, dummy. And you'll see him too.' The Wise Man smiled enigmatically. 'If you really want to.'

'Of course I want to see him!' I said.

And there he was. Standing on the plain not far away,

leading Aladdin behind him as he had done so often. He smiled and waved.

'Don't fear. Trust. And believe!' he shouted. Then he got on Aladdin's back and they rode away. I waved until they had disappeared into the distance.

I really wanted to be with them. Seeing how sad I looked, the Wise Man said: 'The Boy is your best and bravest self. He is always with you. Anyway,' he said, winking, 'they can't work all the time, they need to rest. So do you.'

He laughed at my serious expression. He took my face in his hands and kissed me gently on the forehead.

'Thank you,' he said.

'No, Wise Man,' I replied. 'It is you I should thank. I have learned so much.'

'Oh pshaw,' he said, grinning, 'we've both learned something.'

He put his arm around my shoulder and we walked away.

'One learns something every day,' he said. 'Let me tell you . . . '

And I woke up.

Epilogue

My travels with the Wise Man happened over many nights. After that last night I tried to contact him in my dreams but he never appeared again.

I wondered if it had all been a dream. And yet my sojourn in the other world seemed as real to me as the world I lived in from day to day.

I had filled several journals as I wrote down all that happened to me and my friends on our adventures. And as the Wise Man had asked, I wrote this book and called it 'Travels with a Wise Man'.

I still longed to see the Wise Man again, but he didn't appear.

Sometimes, in my dreams, I would fly with the Boy and Aladdin. And oh, it was wonderful to fly through the air with my friends again. But I was sad we never met the Wise Man. I would always expect to see him but I would usually wake up with a start when I asked about him.

Once the Boy laughed and said: 'You know he always turns up when you least expect it.'

Even though I had written this book, I couldn't help

wondering occasionally if, perhaps, I really had dreamt the whole adventure.

And then one day I was sitting on a park bench, eating a sandwich. I was thinking about nothing in particular, just staring at the ducks on the pond.

A voice said: 'So. How are you, then?'

I turned to see the Wise Man sitting next to me.

'Wise Man!' I said in amazement. 'You are real!'

'Oh pshaw,' he said. 'Did I ever say I wasn't?' He held out his arm. 'Pinch me if you want.'

I did. He grimaced.

'Not so hard.'

I grinned from ear to ear.

'I don't believe this.'

'Oh, you've never had a lot of faith.' But he winked as he said it.

'Well,' he asked. 'When do we begin?'

'Begin?' I said.

'Our travels. I have a little job I want you to do . . . '

And so we began another adventure.

The End

Martin Middleton

Circle of Light

Book One of the Chronicles of the Custodians

'The journey will be hard and many times you will meet Dark forces at work upon this world ... We have awaited your return for centuries, Death Lord ... '

The King of Nuevah is dead, murdered by his own brother, Evil forces threaten to plunge Neuvah into Darkness ... unless a lost prince – ambushed and sold into slavery years before – returns to claim his rightful throne.

Four Vahian soldiers embark on an epic journey in search of the lost prince. They are joined by a young bondservant called Teal, whose instinctive skill with weapons reveals the mystery of his birthright. Teal finds a ring in the subterranean city of Perdu which gives him mystic powers and enables him to draw together others with identical rings and similar abilities. Under Teal's guidance, the seven Usare must use the combined might of the rings to form a Circle of light against the forces of Darkness who threaten to engulf all the lands in war.

Teal's perilous odyssey leads the Usare across many strangelands and sets them against horrifying creatures, savage foes and age-old magic. As they venture closer to the Dark forces, Teal learns of a terrifying ancient prophecy ... that he alone must fulfil.

In the vein of the novels of Raymond E. Feist, Stephen Donaldson and Julian May, *Circle of Light* is a breathtaking combination of fantasy, heroism and adventure, a mythical saga that takes the reader to the very edge of imagination.

Martin Middleton

Triad of Darkness

Book Two of the Chronicles of the Custodians

'And what is the force we must render powerless?'
'The God Erebus – Devourer of Souls.'

The evil that threatens all the lands has not been eliminated by a Peace Treaty, merely temporarily held at bay.

Teal, the hero of *Circle of Light*, is the only one who can stop the Dark forces that hunger for absolute power. He uses the magical abilities he has gained as a Usare – a ring bearer – in his epic struggle with the most dangerous enemies he has yet encountered.

With the help of his Circle of Light, and many new friends, he undertakes a remarkable journey through mythical lands, where he must do battle with the creatures that follow the Darkness . . . and with the Darkness itself.

In this breathtaking fight between good and evil, Teal's odyssey also becomes a journey of discovery, as the truth of his heritage – and his power – is at last revealed.

Martin Middleton

Sphere of Influence

Book Three of the Chronicles of the Custodians

'She is the Darkness . . . She is the underlying evil which has lain upon the world for an eternity, waiting for the first touch of life so She could corrupt it, twist it to Her ways . . . She has decided to use her powers to start a war which neither side can win. And after this war, She will claim the pitiful survivors as Her own.'

Teal the Death Lord, hero of *Circle of Light* and *Triad of Darkness*, has banished the Dark Gods from his world and secured an uneasy peace in the lands under his dominion. But the cost has been great – the Gods of Light have been forced to follow the Gods of Darkness into oblivion. If Teal is to return the Light to his lands, he must also unleash the forces of Darkness and once again do battle with evil.

Teal and his companions set out on a perilous quest for the source of the Darkness. It is this source that Teal must destroy if a time of mass destruction and unparalleled bloodshed is to be averted . . .

In an awesome confrontation between good and evil, Teal comes face to face with his destiny . . . and must make the ultimate sacrifice if he is to curb the Darkness's ever-expanding sphere of influence.

Martin Middleton

The New Age

'The time has come. The New Age is upon us.'

It is over two hundred years since Teal, Death Lord, sacrificed his freedom to imprison the Dark Goddess She in the frozen Pool of Power. The forces of the Light are gone. The Darkness spreads unchecked throughout the land, and its minions plot to free their Goddess.

Only one of the ring-wielding Usare survives. New allies must be found for the Light. Old allegiances are crumbling; new – and unexpected – comrades emerge.

The last of the Usare leads his companions on a perilous quest from the Dark Caverns of the Erg to the oceans beyond the Uskery Sea where, on the Island of the Forgotten Grove, the forces of the Light meet the armies of the Darkness once more . . .

Martin Middleton

The New Order

*'With these rings and weapons he would carve a new
mammon race from the history of old.'*

The Dark Family has been crushed, but the destructive force of Darkness still remains. Under the control of Kaine the Warrior, leader of the New Order of the Mammon, and with the new-found powers of the ancient and powerful Talisman, the mighty hosts of Darkness gather for the ultimate confrontation – to ensure their evil mantle of Darkness reigns in all lands for generations to come.

Undru, the only surviving Janissaire from *The New Age*, and Lyn the Usare Weaver set out with new allies of the Light on a perilous journey through the alien land of a new world to repossess the mythical Talisman . . . towards a breathtaking contest between good and evil.